T0267768

MEET ME IN THE FOURTH DIMENSION

MEET ME IN THE FOURTH DIMENSION

RITA FEINSTEIN

PAGE STREET YA

PAGE STREET YA

Copyright © 2024 Rita Feinstein

First published in 2024 by
Page Street Publishing Co.
27 Congress Street, Suite 1511
Salem, MA 01970
www.pagestreetpublishing.com

Distributed by Macmillan, sales in Canada by The Canadian Manda Group.

28   27   26   25   24   1   2   3   4   5

ISBN-13: 978-1-64567-838-0
ISBN-10: 1-64567-838-5

Library of Congress Control Number: 2023936742

Cover and book design by Emma Hardy for Page Street Publishing Co.
Cover image © Emma Hardy

Printed and bound in China

To my family.

You guys are so weird.

I love you so much.

PREMONITION

The rain has cleared
by the time we reach
the visitor center,
blush-colored clouds
oh-so-perfectly framing
a double rainbow.

This all feels wrong,
but the clusterfucks
of green balloons
tell me this is the right place.

The place the world
will end.

JULY

(SIX MONTHS EARLIER)

THE SUNSPIRIT FESTIVAL

Three days of
face paint and fairy wings,
acrobats and artisans,
puppetry and palmistry.

Three nights of
cider and psilocybin,
drumbeats and didgeridoos,
campfires and confessions.

One moment
that changes everything.

SHANNON AND I

meander the corridors
of lichen-shawled black oaks,
smudging black lipstick
on our tofu burritos.

We're Oregon down to the marrow;
cut us and we'll bleed
blackberries.

Me wicca-as-hell
in a moon phase dress,
silver glitter waxing
and waning down my belly,

and she with her bangles
and Birkenstocks,
her rust-colored hemp dress,
her auburn hair longer
than it's ever been.

She plays the part so well
I almost believe her.

SHANNON NICOLE COLLINS

is my ride(on broomsticks)-or-die,
my neighbor of thirteen years,
the Gemini to my Sagittarius,
the full moon to my eclipse.

Eight years old, sleeping over,
I told her we'd be able to fly
if we leapt from her apple tree
at the stroke of midnight—

a folly that resulted
in a broken wrist for Shannon
and a tongue-lashing for me.

For two weeks, she wasn't
allowed to see me.

What I didn't tell her parents
was that I liked being
her forbidden fruit.

BUT LATELY

she's not biting.

She doesn't want me

to delineate her moon transits

or interpret her dreams.

She wiped away

the dry-erase runes

that repel her older brother

from her bedroom.

She drank instead of danced

her way around

our summer solstice bonfire.

She won't start college

for another month,

but most days it feels

like she's already gone.

THE FIRST INCISION

Something on Shannon's phone
is more interesting than the fifty-foot Chinese dragon
parading down the path.

I lean over to see her school schedule—
Differential Calculus, Molecular Biology,
and something called Physical Geology.

"As opposed to what? Mental Geology?"
I ask, trying to snatch her phone away.

"It's—" She cuts herself off with a sigh.
"Never mind. You don't care."

A pang in my heart. I *do* care,
just not about geology, physical or mental,
or whatever crap they're teaching her.

"Are you sure this is the right schedule?"
I ask. "I think they meant to send this
to someone in the ninth circle of hell."

This, at least, elicits a smile.
"I like science," Shannon says.

Maybe because she didn't have Mr. Byrd
for tenth-grade Biology.

Maybe because she didn't have
an "allergic reaction" to the fixatives
on the crayfish she was dissecting.
That's what the school nurse called it
when I came into her office
with eyes as red as crayfish chitin.

But I knew she was wrong.
I knew what I had *done* was wrong.
Even before my scalpel

made the first incision on the thorax,
I could hear its spirit
crying out in condemnation.

When I accused Mr. Byrd
of causing so much suffering
just for a one-credit science lab,

he laughed and said
the nerve cords of a crayfish
are too primitive for pain.

There's so much
science doesn't know.

"Oh, look," Shannon says,
finally looking up.
"Cool dragon."

AT THE JEWELRY VENDOR

Shannon pauses to admire
a set of malachite earrings.
Mesmerizing green swirls
like an underwater grotto,
sacred, untouchable, pulsing
with forbidden energy.

A powerful healing stone,
recommended only in fragments.

"That's totally your color,"
the artisan says.

Shannon takes out her peridots—
a much friendlier stone—
and slides in the malachites.

A shiver ripples down my spine
as she admires her reflection,
the stones taunting me
as they caress her jawbone.

Their snakelike striations,
their green-on-green gloss,
make me think *secrets.*
Make me think *poison.*

"Are you okay?" I blurt.

Because she must know
what malachite is.
She must be bandaging
a wound I can't see.

Her eyes meet mine in the mirror.
Her smile freezes into a frown.

"Um, yeah? Why wouldn't I be?"
she says, and hands the vendor
a twenty-dollar bill.

I TRY TO FORGET

1. the earrings, how they're shaped
   like upside-down obelisks,
   monuments to a dark future

2. the end of summer
   crouched in the dry grass,
   creeping closer on unsheathed claws

3. the pale band on Shannon's finger
   where my hematite ring
   once shielded her from harm

FESTIVAL GIRL

I grew up in Sunspirit, running barefoot
between stilt-walkers' legs,
clapping soap bubbles
to sparkly smithereens.

Most years, my mom runs a booth
where she sells herbal tinctures
and moon-infused water,
but this year

her Volvo's alternator overheated,
the goldenseal rotted in its bed,
and a snake on the garden path
told her to stay home.

"Everything happens for a reason,"
she said with a shrug,
waving me off as I climbed
into Shannon's Jeep.

Everything happens—a wide-open
night sky of possibility—
for a reason—a pattern, a purpose
in every scattering of stars.

But Shannon's glassy smiles
and wine-dark silences
and tepid shrugs:
I can't decipher them.

SHADOWS

seep honey-slow
between the trees,

sunset guttering
like a lavender candle.

Last bows are taken,
last kombuchas poured

as the fair shuts down for the night,
but I'm not ready for anything

to end, so on our way
back to the campsite,

I grab Shannon's wrist
and point at a brocaded tent.

Palm Readings, $5

WE'VE READ OUR FORTUNES

in star charts and tarot cards,
tea leaves and thrown bones.

We've chalked the pentagrams,
swung the pendulums.

We've looked for ourselves
everywhere but our own bodies.

SHANNON GOES FIRST

which is a first.

I'm six months older, six decibels louder.
The first to call and the first to hang up,
the first to wake at every sleepover.

I'm the one who snuck over her fence,
cutting myself on brambles and nettles,
the nights we weren't allowed to see each other.

I'm the high priestess of our two-witch coven,
yelling when she incants a spell wrong
or breaks her applewood wand.

But I'm trying to be better.
I'm trying not to hold
on so tight.

If she flies away,
I want to be the roost
she always returns to.

CRUEL TOPOGRAPHY

Shannon emerges from the tent,
blushing guiltily.

She shows me her head line,
how it runs parallel to her life line
before veering away, then forking
up toward her Mount of Mercury.

A call to travel, to independence,
to a college 1,500 miles away.

Her palm becomes a map,
her veins West Coast highways,
her blood cells taillights

disappearing into the dark.

INSIDE THE TENT

it's dark, cramped, and humid—
sweet with sandalwood incense.

The palmist sits on a floor pillow
in front of a long, low table.
She's fifty-ish and dressed simply
in a t-shirt and jeans, her black hair
swept into a ponytail.

I sit cross-legged across from her.
The rays of the setting sun
angling through the tent flaps
leave hot lines on my back.

The palmist inspects my hand
like a jeweler appraising a gem.

"Has anyone told you
about your life line?"
she asks.

I shake my head and wait
for her to explain,
but she just goes, "Mmh."

Her almond-shaped nail
traces a crease on my palm,
and my skin tickles helplessly.

"Do you know," she asks,
"where your north node is?"

THE NORTH NODE

is the point where the moon's orbit
intersects with the sun's apparent path
at the moment of your birth.

"It shows what you're supposed to do
so that your soul can evolve," Shannon said,
that summer night we taught ourselves
to transcribe the firmament into symbols.

Sitting cross-legged on her trampoline,
Astrology.com printouts spread on the canvas,
we read interpretations to each other
by the bluelight of our phones.

"Yours is in Virgo," she said, "which means
you're supposed to be helping people.
And you can start by getting me another La Croix."

I rolled my eyes. "And your destiny
is ordering me around?"

She flashed me a wicked grin.
"That's why we're perfect for each other."

DESTINY'S HORSESHOE

Flung by fate, my north node
had clanged to a stop in my twelfth house.

The palmist nods like she was expecting this.

"Our souls travel counterclockwise
through the zodiac with each lifetime—"
she sketches a circle in the air,
"—from first house to twelfth."

A smile softens her face.
The stub of her incense stick
crumbles to ash.

She folds my fingers inward
and gives my fist a gentle squeeze.

"You're at the end," she says,
"of your soul's journey."

THE END?

i
feel
like
i'm
just
beg-
inning

RITA FEINSTEIN

by the time I rejoin Shannon.

"What's wrong?" she asks,
and I almost laugh because
that's what I've been too afraid
to ask her, because if it's something
I did, something I *am*,
I don't want to know.

So I say, "nothing,"
but my hand burns
where the palmist touched me
and wiping it on my dress
just spreads the fire,
and when have I ever
kept secrets from Shannon?

"Well, actually," I say,
and relay the palmist's words.

Shannon picks at her nails,
painted a shade of blue I like
only when she's wearing it.

"That's a good thing, right?"
she says. "You beat the game."

Which just makes me think of
the hours we spent in her den,
taking turns with the Switch controller,
sweaty hands jamming buttons
in the boss fight,

how we screamed and hugged each other
when Link destroyed Calamity Ganon,

then silently drifted apart
as the end credits rolled.

I'VE ALWAYS HATED SUNSET

As we leave the fairgrounds,
I mutter the time-freezing incantation
Shannon and I tried to extend our playdates with.

Once, we thought we'd succeeded—
turned out her microwave clock was just broken.

Time doesn't congeal now, either.
If anything, it flows faster—

last night of the fair

last day of summer

last time I see Shannon

college

job hunt

marriage

kids

retirement

death

and then nothing.

NORTHWESTERN NOCTURNE

We walk across the two-lane highway,
its shoulders thick with Queen Anne's lace.

A dead toad is smeared across the asphalt—
one voice snuffed from the night choir

that greets us in hoots and chirps and moans
as we push through curtains of lichen,

our path lit by the hazy moon
shining down through the sugar pines,

and oh, Oregon, Oregon,
how could Shannon ever leave you?

Real and 8-bit pioneers died of dysentery
trying to reach you.

Oregon, your riverbanks veiled with
bleeding heart and sour salmonberry,

your forests rich with wood sorrel
and wild grape, trilliums and meadowfoam,

your coastline rubbed raw with salt,
your beaches strewn with moon jellies.

Oregon, when I press my ear against
your mossy carpet, I hear your heartbeat—

when did Shannon go deaf?
The worst part isn't that she wants to leave,

it's that she didn't seem to care either way,
and I couldn't convince her to stay.

RELEASED

The fair lives again at night:
a pop-up village of tents and Volkswagen vans.
The air smells like hickory smoke, yellow curry,
and the damp, compost-y tang of Oregon soil.

Shannon wants to lie down, but there's something
teeming termite-like under my skin,
some energy that needs to be released—
I want to dance barefoot, to sing until I scream,

so I drag her to the nearest campfire,
where a topless woman with painted breasts
hands us hard cider and beaded bongos,
neither of which Shannon touches,

and when I get up to dance, she just
gazes abstractedly into the woods,
her earrings glinting menacingly
in the firelight, and I think about

how we were having a perfect day
until she bought the damn things,
and I want to rip them from her head
and cast them into the hot coals—

but she's already walking away,
her sandals slapping the dirt.
Breathless, I catch her
before she slips inside our tent.

Her swinging earrings mock me,
disaster bells only I can hear.

WHAT I SAY TO SHANNON

Wait. Stop. Talk to me.

You can tell me anything—
you know that, right?

You must've picked those earrings
for a reason. You know it's only
for deep wounds, don't you?

So, either something's wrong,
or it's going to go wrong,

or you're just using this powerful stone
for ornamentation.

But can't you feel it?
Its energy?

How can you even let it touch you?

And that dead toad we saw—
if that's not a fucking omen,
I don't know what is.

You're not losing your Sight . . .
are you?

Because maybe there's a blockage
in your third eye chakra,
but we can fix that!
We just need to swap the malachite
for quartz or amethyst.

Something for clarity and purification.

We can go back to the jeweler tomorrow.

You'll be okay, Shannon.

I lost my Sight in eighth grade, remember?
But it comes back.

You're just having a dry spell.
But I can help you—

WE'RE NOT WITCHES

Shannon says.

She puts "witches" in air quotes,
four little daggers,
one for each chamber of my heart.

"Not everything is an omen, Crosby.
Not everything means something."

There's a new edge in her voice,
so sharp I taste copper.

"We can't do this anymore," she says,
"I never believed in this stuff anyway,"

and in renouncing her powers,
she casts a spell that shatters me.

"I bought the earrings because I like them.
And I'm keeping them," she says

before disappearing into the tent.

LARGER VOICES CALLING

Midnight finds me wandering the campground,
my skirt heavy with sweat and thistleheads,
my aura bitter-black like gas station coffee.

I don't understand how Shannon could turn
her back on me, on all the memories
I thought we shared.

Gathering herbs by moonlight,
interpreting symbols in our dreams,
warding off demons with salt circles—

none of that means anything to her?

What about the time we summoned
her cat's spirit from its cremated remains?

What about the time the bus bullies
stopped throwing pencil lead at us
after we put their names in the freezer?

My mind whirls through explanations—
she's jealous that I have
the keener Sight

her parents have finally
turned her against me

her stupid science summer camp
taught her truth is something
you perceive with your five
(and *only* five) senses

I'm the dog in the sad dog movie,
and she's only throwing stones
because goodbye is too painful—

But my mind stills
as a familiar song spills chills
down my spine.

Think about how many times I have fallen,
spirits are using me, larger voices calling.

I follow the music to an older couple,
her voice as bright and clear as the stars,
his guitar as warm and vital as their campfire.

She looks up and locks eyes with me
as she sings the last line of the bridge:

What heaven brought you and me cannot be forgotten—

SOUTHERN CROSS

My parents grew up
with glitter and grunge,
synthpop and glam rock,
mullets and metallics,
spandex and shoulder pads,

but they belonged
in a different decade,
playing folk music
and weaving flower crowns—

which is how in 2001,
at a Crosby, Stills & Nash show
in Eugene, Oregon,
surrounded by old hippies,
dancing to a song about how
the universe heals all pain,

they found each other,
and how four years later
at their daughter's waterbirth,
they knew exactly what to name her.

I DON'T BELIEVE IN COINCIDENCE

A path that crosses
will cross again.

Every encounter is a stitch
in a larger tapestry.

So I'm surprised (but not)
to recognize the singing woman
as the palmist who read
a dead end in my skin,

and she doesn't say
I've been expecting you
or some shit,
but she does invite me
to sing along if I know the words,

and when her partner
has strummed the final chords,
she points coyly
at a yellow-white star,
like it will burst into flight
if I move too suddenly.

"Deva," she says,
and it's a good ten seconds
before I realize we're back on earth,
and she's telling me her name.

DEVA REVATHI

runs a small psychic practice in Corvallis,
where I'll be starting college next month.

(The threads of fate tighten, the pattern
of its cat's cradle becoming clearer.)

Her companion—Grateful Dead bears marching
across his tie-dye tank top—goes by Bear.

With a grin wider than his mustache,
he time-travels three decades into the future

on his guitar frets, this time playing Taylor Swift's
"We Are Never Ever Getting Back Together,"

and we drama-queen our way through the song,
every note wrong, every word right,

and this, *this*, is where I want to be,
the tideline between pop culture and spirit,

obscene and divine, mystical and mundane,
but the tideline isn't a place. It's a choice—

bury your toes in reality,
or get swept out to sea.

MY TYPE

Deva and Bear are obviously in love
                              with the stars.

The fleck of white-gold
swanning across the low horizon
is Venus, planet of pleasure.

"Where's your friend?" Deva asks.
                    "Or girlfriend?"

Girlfriend—ha. Shannon isn't my type.
Which is to say   human.

Follow me to the forest path
at twilight, and I'll show you
how the brambles look like fingers
reaching up from Tír na nÓg,

how if you look with your heart
and not your eyes, you can see them—
sloe-eyed and antler-crowned,
algae-green and androgynous,
mossy smiles hungry for me.

Lose me   find me   seven years later
waking up in a circle of mushrooms,
a gentle smile on my face

as I walk back into the brambles
and beg them to take me
for another seven.

SHANNON'S TYPE

is Xavier Black—
who carries around a tattered *1984* paperback,
always smells like blue raspberry vape juice,
and is trying to bring tinted sunglasses back—

because he let her keep the pen
she'd borrowed in AP Lit.

Weston Humphries—
the short, mousy kid who doesn't own
a single non-Minecraft-themed shirt
and has volcanic flows of acne on both cheeks—

because one year for Secret Santa,
he got Shannon an Olive Garden gift card.

And let's not forget Drew Carpenter—
God-fearing, trophy-hunting, corn-shucking
mama's boy, famous only for shitting his pants
after eating eight cafeteria corndogs—

because when Shannon twisted her ankle
before gymnastics regionals,
he said he'd pray for her.

That's all it took.
A pen.
A gift card.
A prayer.

I've given her everything,
and she gives herself to anyone
who gives her anything.

WHAT STAR IS THAT?

Bear asks, pointing at the vertex of the firmament.
The star's greenish gleam reminds me
of the glow-in-the-dark ones on the bunk bed
Shannon had all to herself,
how I thumbed them off while she slept
and arranged them into more auspicious constellations.

The more you fuck with fate,
the less adhesive it becomes.

"I think you'll have to name it," Deva says.

"And I think Crosby should do the honors,"
Bear says, giving me a courtly bow.

As if naming something is easy.
As if names aren't invocations.
When you speak a fairy's name,
you bind it to your will.

"Shannon," I say,

the two syllables so sharp
that I hear the sticky rip
of wax paper peeling from glue

as I give her a permanent,
phosphorescent place
in my universe.

A FEW SONGS AND STARS LATER

I say good night, uncreak my knees,
and make my way back through the dark.

Most campfires have been extinguished
and nothing looks familiar.

My heart climbs farther up my throat
with each passing tent that isn't ours.

It's after midnight, July 12
bleeding over into July 13—

bad luck, bad night
to be alone,

bad idea to name dead light
after someone I'm afraid to lose.

I want to take it back, want to wrest
Shannon's name from the green star's teeth,

but it winks at me
like it's already swallowed.

MARKED

Finally I find it: the little two-person tent
that Shannon and I used to pitch
in the field behind her house
on summer nights,

the memories so crisp
that when I open the flap,
I see our third-grade selves

making arts and crafts
with glitter-gluey fingers,
shrieking with laughter
when her brother Aaron

lumbered around the tent
like a bear, then pawed inside
to tickle Shannon

until I scribbled pink marker
all over his face
and he sullenly retreated
back across the lawn—

I blink and the memories dissipate.
Shannon lies motionless on the ground,
facing away from me. Unbreathing,

I watch for the gentle rise and fall
of her sleeping bag
before allowing myself
to crawl inside my own.

Sleep won't come easy.
Something sinister is shadow-dancing
across the tent nylon,

toying with the zipper.
This time, I'll arm myself with something
sharper than a pink marker. This time,
I won't let anyone else inside.

AUBADE

The sky through the tent mesh is lint-blue
and embroidered with birdsong,

the muzzy dawn-light falling
on Shannon's empty sleeping bag.

AUGUST

GO BEAVS!

OSU, our hats are off to you

               Because my parents couldn't afford a private school

Beavers, Beavers, fighters through and through

               I picked the state school with the least stupid mascot

We'll root for every man, we'll cheer for every stand

               not like you'll catch me dead at a football game.

That's made for old OSU.

               Campus a tidy redbrick Lego set

Watch our team go tearing down the field

               plastic sorority girls fundraising for trending #tragedies

Men of iron, their strength will never yield.

               while plastic frat boys marinate in Natty Lite.

Hail, hail, hail, hail

               Hell goes by another name here—

Hail to old OSU.

               freshman orientation icebreakers.

SUMMONING SPELL: SCHOOL SPIRIT

A circle of candles to conjure.
A circle of salt to protect.
A circle of students
                    to waste everyone's fucking time.

In the circle's bull's-eye
(right where the demon would appear),
a student ambassador in a neon orange t-shirt
bends us to her will.

"We have common ground," she yells,
"if you play a sport."

Laughing and shrieking, several kids scatter
across the summer-parched lawn.

The student ambassador
takes the empty spot next to me,
beaming a smile I don't return.

A kid in a *Jurassic Park* t-shirt,
the last one in the middle,
issues the next command.

"We have common ground," he lisps,
"if you're wearing sandals."

I beg the grass to swallow my feet,
but "go, go, go!" the ambassador yells,
shoving me forward.

A witch on parade to the stake or gallows
has nothing left but her dignity.
I don't run   I walk.

Exasperated, the ambassador
summons me to the center.

My turn
to burn.

WE HAVE COMMON GROUND

If you keep seeing magpies in fours.

If the cord of your amethyst necklace—the one you haven't taken off since middle school—snapped this morning.

If you keep drawing the Wheel of Fortune, the most useless card because all it means is that whatever happens next is up to fate.

If your dorm room has terrible feng shui and now you need to buy some mirrors and prisms to make the chi flow properly.

If your best friend hasn't talked to you in a month.

If your soul is in its last cycle before evaporating.

If you're the only one who can hear the slow, grinding approach of something nameless and terrible.

UNCOMMON GROUND

My voice sticks in my throat.
I can already tell I don't have anything
in common with these people.

But not every witch
has white hair and black lipstick.
A kindred spirit might be hiding
inside one of these Maddysons or Mackenzeighs.

"We have common ground if you read tarot cards,"
I say into a bottomless void.

No one moves.

"What?" someone yells.

I repeat myself,
but still the circle holds.

"What's another fun fact about you?"
the ambassador prompts.

I grit my teeth.
I'd hardly call my lifelong dedication
to deciphering the mysteries of the universe
a *fun fact*.

"We have common ground if you're vegetarian,"
I concede, and this time, one or two kids run.

The ambassador gives me a patronizing thumbs-up,
and I whisper a hex under my breath.

Hope she likes nightmares,
because now it's *her* turn to run.

THE BACK-TO-SCHOOL BBQ

is a sad affair of foods I can't—or won't—eat:
overcooked burgers, undercooked chicken wings,
a mostly-mayo coleslaw, and watermelon wedges
so mealy they fall right off the rind.

Good idea, watermelon. I collapse
into a folding chair at the far corner
of the canopy tent, so far uninfected
by my normie-ass peers.

I slip my feet from my sandals
and bury my toes in the hot grass,
but there's no pulse—the whole of
Willamette Valley has flatlined.

Back home, in the verdant foothills
of the coastal range,
the worse the radio reception,
the stronger the earth's energy.

A dark thought eclipses my mind—
what if it's not the signal that's weak,
but the instrument?
What if it's me?

I touch my amethyst, then run my fingers
up the cord to the hasty knot I tied
when I stood up this morning
and my crystal heart clattered to the ground.

I won't lose myself here.
I won't lose myself here.
But people don't always lose themselves.
Sometimes they just fall out of reach.

TEAGAN

My roommate, ladies and gentlemen.

Observe her unsolicited hugging and Instagramming,
how she's already posted six nonconsensual photos of me.

Observe how, characteristic of her species
(white upper-middle-class suburban Oregon teenager),
she's dressed in moisture-wicking athleisurewear
that's never wicked a drop of moisture.

Observe—and then quickly look away from—
the delicate gold crucifix around her neck.
That's gonna be a problem.

Observe her décor as it goes up:
two whole corkboards of polaroids and ticket stubs,
a life-size cardboard Harry Styles,
posters with in—substantial—spirational sayings like
the best things in life aren't things.

Observe the port-wine stain
like a handprint cupping her jaw.
She's probably self-conscious about it,
but it's the only thing I like about her.

Now let's give her a big round of applause,
ladies and gentlemen, as she recites her lines flawlessly:
"Wanna go to a party tonight?"

THE WHEEL OF FORTUNE

Parties aren't really my thing
unless I'm sweeping in unannounced
to place a curse on a newborn princess.

"It's a nerd party," she reassures me,
"at my nerd brother's house."

Bailey's a grad student living off campus
with two Maine Coon cats and three housemates—
one in nuclear physics, one in computer science,
and one in fermentation science:

"—which is literally just a beer major,"
Teagan explains, and with a wink and a nudge,
she singsongs, "I hear he's got a new brew."

I can't be tempted. I haven't even purified
the dorm yet. There's an unlit sage stick
in my suitcase just waiting to chase
the bad spirits from the corners.

"And it's a potluck," Teagan adds.

Okay, I *can* be tempted.
My dinner—a cup of lemonade—
is now just high-fructose sludge
coating my stomach.

I think about the Wheel,
about trusting in where it lands,
and suddenly, for just a moment,
I feel like I've stopped spinning.

LEAVING THE DORM

feels like breaking out of prison.
Pretty sure our building
was once a bomb shelter
or the kind of mental hospital
where they boarded up gay people
in bathtubs full of freezing water.

Beyond the automatic doors
is a hideous abstract sculpture,
a sea anemone in eternal torment,
metal tentacles hot from the sun,
which is just beginning to set
behind the distant coastal range,
the only home I'll ever know.

Through the bleed of light,
a green eye opens—the same star
that's been watching me since the palmist
traced my shattered life line
and whispered *the end*.

PLATITUDES

Where are you from?

nameless stretch of highway
in the Lorane backwoods /
purple house hand-painted
with suns and moons / lawn strewn
with figs and antler velvet

cul-de-sac in south Eugene /
yellow split-level / 4 bedroom
3 bath / gorgeous natural light /
backyard swing set / prize-
winning orchids

What are your hobbies?

walking barefoot in the forest /
swimming naked in the creek

PSLs with BFFs
singing to / for / about God

What do you want to study?

pre-Christian religion /
Western esotericism

maybe psychology

Tell me about your necklace.

it was my grandmother's

it was my grandmother's

Despite Teagan's briefing, I expected more boys
in pink polos, more girls in fast-fashion crop tops,
the air filled with bone-quaking bass
and the smell of flat-ironed hair.

But this party fits a different stereotype,
a kind of scripted hipsterdom:

Fantastic Mr. Fox playing with no volume,
half-finished game of Catan on the coffee table,
portable speaker moaning boneless indie music.

A dozen strangers stare at me.

One of whom—with his elfin features
and dark crop of curls—can only be
Teagan's brother.

     I know him
from *High School Musical*—
a pretty boy with no real problems.

"Gross," he says, "a freshman."

Teagan punches his shoulder,
making some beer slosh
from his *I Love My ~~Husband~~ Dog* mug.

"Okay, senior citizen," she says,
"how 'bout you get us some beer
before your knees give out?"

"Jeez, T, respect your elders."
He winks at me. "Right, Grandma?"

GRANDMA

An unoriginal nickname for a kid
who went gray in seventh grade.

I've heard it all—

"Tell me about World War II."
"Tell me about the dinosaurs."
"Tell me about the Big Bang."

Once, the class idiot tried to prove
I had false teeth, but instead of dentures,
his fingers came away with blood.

Shannon's pediatrician mom
figured I was malnourished
or immunocompromised.

She wouldn't understand
that magic has a cost,
and I pay in pigment.

Every spell cast
is another streak
of snow.

BLACKOUT

A Lorane party
is backwoods AF,
boys knee-deep in the creek
trawling for crayfish,
and always some idiot
waiting to scare the crap out of you
when you drunk-stumble
into the woods to piss.

Here, instead of bonfire stories
about ghost loggers with chainsaw hands,
kids exchange "is it cake?" TikToks
and echo chamber opinions
about this fall's election.

At least the beer is good—
watermelon gose, they call it,
sour and salty with a cheeky pucker.
It eases the pressure,
silences the warning bells,

soothes the hurt at how no one
asks about my amethyst
or my black lipstick
or the tattoo of the Sagittarius glyph
on my left shoulder.

I didn't cast invisibility,
but no one seems to see me.

DOWN TO EARTH

Back to the wall, I observe the party
        as if from a great height,
                high and getting higher

as the alcohol inflates my head
        like a hot-air balloon
                fed by a golden flame,

beautifully, tragically alone
        in the upper atmosphere,
                ice-cold and altitude-sick

until Teagan appears like ballast,
        pulling me back to earth
                and passing me an iPhone,

asking me to queue the next song,
        and my heart plays
                a max-volume memory

of Shannon driving us to Sunspirit,
        one hand on the steering wheel and
                the other handing me her phone,

saying, "*not* 'Baby Shark,'"
        and me grinning because I didn't know
                it was the last song I'd ever pick for her,

and now Teagan is smiling expectantly,
        not even considering the stupid shit
                I'm capable of, not knowing

how I could fill the air with discord
        as easily as clicking "play next,"
                but this time I don't—

I don't want to scare away
        this girl who has been nothing
                except kind to me—

so I pick an indie song that I know
        will go down smooth as this beer,
                which Teagan affirms

with an "ooh, good choice,"
        before floating back into the crowd
                and leaving me here,
                        alone and
                                out of reach.

THE SONG AFTER MINE

is a screamy metal nightmare
that lurches up my brainstem like a jump-scare.

Only one person seems to be enjoying it,
some dude in a Free Cascadia t-shirt.
I'm all for inventing a new, better country,
but I've never put much credence in the Pacific Northwest
seceding from the union—a revolution that exists
purely in bong smoke and Facebook groups.

He headbangs his way over to the snack table
and gives me a curious once-over.

"Sick tat," he says, and though I wish
I could power-wash my eardrums,
I'm pleased someone noticed.

"Are you a witch?" he asks, and I say yes
because my forebears busted their asses
so we wouldn't have to live in the shadows.

And when he says, "I'm a Satanist,"
I don't laugh or wrinkle my nose
because when people tell you who they are,
you should believe them.

He scratches his patchy goatee
and speaking of goats,
that's the kind of blood you have to drink
in a ritual for siphoning life force.

I take a nervous gulp of watermelon beer.
"Have you ever done it?"

"Two confirmed kills," he deadpans,

and that's when I realize
from an eruption of nearby giggles
that he's fucking with me.

SMALL-TOWN WITCH

I burn down to embarrassed ashes,
then flare to my feet
and into the backyard,
where evening has bruised into night,
tender to the touch.

Flopping onto the flagstones
that ring a brackish goldfish pond,
I drain the dregs of lukewarm beer,
wishing Satan would refill
my solo cup with goat blood.

Feverish heat licks my temples.
Unshed tears stopper my throat.

I feel someone looking at me,
but it's just a plaster statue
of Godzilla devouring a garden gnome.

Back home I was feared, followed
through the convenience store
as I browsed bottled iced coffees.

Parents whispered prayers
behind my back, thinking—what?
I'd curdle their cows' milk?
Break their daughters' hymens?

I was uninvited from birthday parties,
assigned unspeaking roles in school plays.
I was a threat, not a joke.

I bare my teeth at Godzilla,
but he doesn't look up from his dinner.

GO FISH

Up to my elbows,
up to my shoulders
in the pond, I search
for answers but
find only algae.

"I have some fish sticks
in the freezer," a voice says,
and I startle with a splash.
"Those might be easier to catch."

AN INVITATION

"You're right," Bailey says,
even though I didn't say anything.
"This party sucks. Too bad
the sword-swallowers and lion tamers
had to cancel. And what's with this playlist?"
He yells over his shoulder,
"Play Taylor Swift, you cowards!"

"Never!" someone yells from the back porch.

I'm supposed to quirk a grateful smile,
thank you thank you for cheering me up,
but I am neither cheered nor grateful.

When a girl walks away,
why does a guy
see it as an invitation?

Bailey's smile drops *kerplunk*
into the fishpond, and he sits beside me,
all deerlike legs and coral-colored shorts.

"Sorry about Joshua," he says.
"He's basically wasted all the time,
so you can just ignore him."

I feel a twinge of guilt for being
so high-maintenance, for not being
able to take some light teasing.

"I was just getting some fresh air,"
I mumble.

"It's a nice night," Bailey says,

and I 99 percent disagree with him,
but the other 1 percent is the valley sky,
wide open and blazing with stars
that I couldn't see from the heart
of the dense Siuslaw Forest.

Bailey follows my eyes to the heavens,
then gets back to his feet.
"Follow me," he says. "There's something
I want to show you."

BAILEY TAKES ME TO HIS ROOM

Should I be worried?
Is the thing he wants to show me
his dick?

This doesn't seem like the kind of party
where you get raped,
but I mutter a protective spell
as we walk up the stairs.

His room smells like mildew and Old Spice.
Drifts of clothes on the floor,
posters of nebulae on the walls,
a telescope hanging halfway out the window.

Not a dick, but close enough.

THE LAST TIME I USED A TELESCOPE

was never.

Astrology is the only lens
I've viewed the cosmos through.

Bailey's wide eyes are Uranian blue,
zapping me with disbelief.

"Neil deGrasse Tyson literally just died
so that he could roll over in his grave,"

he says, and maybe that's what I want—
to be the girl with science's blood on her hands,

but I also want to see through an eye
five hundred times stronger than my own.

Looking through the eyepiece
is like going underwater.

I hold my breath as Bailey whispers,
somewhere light-years behind me,

"Do you see it? The green one?
That's Malachite."

MALACHITE

I stumble away from the telescope.
Nausea tidal-waves through me
as my vision struggles to adjust.
Everything seems much too close.

"M-Malachite?"

Shannon's earrings.
A warning.
A wound.

Bailey mirrors my confusion,
like he can't believe I don't
follow NASA on Twitter.

"A rogue dwarf planet," he explains,
breathy with awe. "It's on the outskirts
of our solar system now, but in January
it'll be passing through Venus's orbit."

Deep in my brain, something clicks
and keeps clicking, a bomb clock
counting down.

"Want another look?" Bailey asks,
but I've seen enough.

A dark-green orb emerging
from the waters of deep space,
smoldering in the light of a nameless sun,
turning its faceless face toward Earth.

TOO CLOSE

At its closest

Malachite will be

38 million kilometers

away from Earth.

There is no chance

there is no chance

that we will collide.

MAL–

To the naked eye, it's no bigger
than a fleck of body glitter,
but I've lost all perspective.

Sometimes you don't know how big
something is, how fast it's traveling,
until it hits you.

Sometimes you give a star
your best friend's name,
and it throws it back in your face.

Malachite—the reptilian bite
of its syllables, the way it forces
you to bare your teeth.

Can't Bailey hear its dissonant whisper?
Can't he think of other words
that start with *mal*?

This isn't a planet; it's a message.
I don't know what it means,
but I know it's bad.

I HAVE TO CALL SHANNON

i gasp   pushing past Bailey

    down the stairs

                 through the sleeping streets

phone sweating   against my ear

                  pick up   pick up   pick up   pick up

dehydration headache   firing a gun   into my temple

    stars raining down   on me like glass

                  pick up   pick up   pick up   pick up

same star i saw   the night   shannon walked away from me

          pick up   pick up   pick up   pick up   pick—

                      "Hello?"

HER VOICE

is heartbreakingly familiar,
a softness you can only achieve
with lavender laundry detergent.

There's a whole planet in my throat,
and I struggle to swallow.

"Are you okay?" I choke out.

"I'm fine. Are *you* ok—"

"Do you know about Malachite?"

Silence. Gentle murmurs
like swaying seaweed in the background.
Who is she with?

"Now actually isn't a good time,"
she says. "Can I call you back
in like an hour?"

It's 10:44 now.

I walk aimlessly,
past the 24-hour Safeway,
through a graffitied skate park,
along the Willamette River,
while Malachite inches closer
to Earth's orbit.

At midnight, Shannon still hasn't called.

NECROMANCY

My head is a beehive
wadded with pollen,
thick and dripping
and angrily abuzz.

When I open my eyes,
I'm lobotomized
by white-hot pokers
of sunlight.

Water. I need water.
Hydrate or die-drate.

I reanimate my corpse out of bed,
shamble to the coed bathroom,
cup my hands under two different faucets
before a motion sensor notices me.

My tastebuds recoil like barnacles
at the warm water's sulfurous taste.
I race my upset stomach to the toilet
and win by a split second.

Four watermelon beers lighter,
I stagger back to the mirror.
Lipstick an oily smear,
mascara hysterically smudged.

A half-dead thing
on her last life.

ABLAZE

Back in our room, Teagan is awake and preening
in the mirror, straightening and re-curling her curls.
In her white dress and sleeveless denim jacket,
she looks like she's auditioning for *The Voice*
specifically to impress Blake Shelton.

"Wow, you look like the nuclear engineering kids
have been experimenting on you," she says.

I faceplant into bed. "Just hungover."

I can hear the lie in the gallows-creak
of my voice. I've been doubly poisoned
by alcohol and a summer cold.

My light-sensitive eyes flicker
to the unlit sage stick on my dresser.
Maybe if I had cleansed the dorm
instead of going to that stupid party,
I could've warded off the sickness.

Teagan sets her curling iron down.
Her perfect eyebrows furrow with concern.
"Do you need to go to the health center?"

"No, really. I'm fine." My body
can handle this on its own.

But my forehead is blazing, and not
in an awakened-sixth-chakra way.

My phone is blazing too—a text from my mom
wishing me a happy first day of classes.

Fuck.

None of my mom's holistic healing books
mention college algebra as a cure
for aches and chills, so I don't go.

As the sun climbs up the unshaded window,
prying bright fingers under my eyelids,
I remember my mom sitting next to me
on the living room couch as I watched
an episode of *The Magic School Bus*
where the kids watch a white blood cell
devouring a germ, and she told me,
"You know it's not all real, right?"

and I nodded because I was five years old
and I knew cartoons were just drawings,
but then she explained that "the pathogen
is nothing; the terrain is everything,"
and that if I am a vigilant caretaker
of my body's garden, nothing can burrow
through my soil, nothing can consume
my blooms or suck the sap from my veins.

Sorry, Mom. I've been a shit caretaker.
My body is more garbage than garden.

I need to irrigate, but the tap water
tastes like Satan's ass crack,
and Teagan's 24-pack of Dasanis
is all the way across the room.

Morning turns to noon turns to night.
My brain boils in my skull.
I fall asleep with the imagined kiss
of moon-infused water on my lips.

FEVER DREAMS

skipping stones   in the coffee-colored Siuslaw River

the rock in my hand   green   striped darker-green

released too soon   it smashes   into Shannon's mouth

green stone   white bone   slicked red

nine planets   perfect as buttons   in the twilight

bigger   closer   than the moon

Mom crying as she drives   to the bank   the bank is closed

not like any amount of money   could pay the sky

not to come   crashing down

I'M AWAKE

and something is wrong.
Someone is screaming.
Someone is shaking
my shoulder, and I think

about that scene in *Bambi*
where the Prince of the Forest,
silhouetted by flames,
rumbles, "you *must* get up,"

and Bambi gets up, so I
do too, letting Teagan
pull me out the door
even though antlers

of pain are branching
from my forehead,
and I have a cold
naked feeling at my throat

where my amethyst
snapped off again,
and I was wrong—
I'm not the deer

but the fire,
blackening everything,
everyone fleeing
like pheasants

from my touch.

JUST A DRILL

The only fire is the controlled burn
of my white blood cells.

The night is a warm bath
that might as well be
the ice bucket challenge.

I turn back toward the lobby,
but the RA blocks my path,
saying we need to wait
for campus security
to give the all clear.

Alarms still singeing my ears,
I find a place away from the crowd
to slump against the brick wall

and close my eyes for a moment—

AND THEN A VOICE FROM ABOVE SAYS

"Hey. Hey, kid.
You alright, kid?
Need me to call someone?"

The voice is coming from
six campus security officers
with identical buzzcuts.

No, wait—just one officer.
I blink to bring him
into groggy focus.

"Party a little too hard?"
he asks. One of his eyes
is blue, the other lazy.

When I stand up,
I get a colorful headrush,
my vision spray-painted maroon.

"You a freshman?" he asks.
Like that explains everything.

He steps forward.
I step back.

"I'm okay. Really. Sorry.
I'll go back to my room now."

"I'd feel much better
if you went to the health center."

The steel in his voice tells me
it's not a feeling; it's a command.

"I just need to lie down,"
I say meekly.

He shakes his head.
"My dad said the same thing
before his heart attack.

Come on, kid,
I'll give you a ride."

was inspired by the waiting room
of OSU's student health center.

The lobby's aggressive air conditioning
slaps me back into lucidity.

I'm stuccoed in goose bumps,
shivering in my hard plastic chair,

tortured by the tinny speakers
taunting me with "Teenage Dream."

Fear punctures my stomach
when the doctor calls my name.

I've never been to a hospital,
never had a shot, never felt this alone.

"So what's going on?" she asks
as I sit on her paper-covered table.

Her voice is petal-soft and kind
and puts me immediately on edge.

I can't let her manipulate me
into taking something I don't need.

"It's just a cold," I say,
and she says, "Mmh."

I feel stupid and childish
holding the thermometer under my tongue.
I have a 101.3° fever.
She offers Tylenol and Nyquil,

and my mind plays the nope-nope-nope
octopus gif on repeat.

"No thanks. I can . . . I have stuff I can take."
Technically not true, but I know what to get.

All I need is echinacea, lemon, honey, cayenne,
and the tea mug I made from river clay.

Even through her mask, I can see her smile fade.
"I'd feel a little better if you took some now."

I'd feel better.

I'd feel better if I forced you into my car.
If I forced you into a drugged stupor.

She's just like the campus security fuckhead,
protocol masquerading as sympathy.

As soon as *I don't want to be here* crosses my mind,
I realize *I don't have to be here.*

I'm eighteen years old, a fucking adult.
I can come and go as I please.

"Could I possibly have a glass of water?" I ask.
As soon as she's gone, I slip out the door and into the night.

TEAGAN AMBUSHES ME

with a fierce hug
and a dozen questions,

and something slugs me
in the gut because

I know if the situation
were reversed,

if she were the one
who disappeared,

I would have gone
right back to sleep.

CHROMOTHERAPY

Periwinkle — the predawn sky when I wake up
smelling like a bar & grill

Lavender — the deodorant I slather under my arms

Turmeric — the same deep, anti-inflammatory yellow
as my favorite corduroys

Black — for protection, for deflection, for absorbing
my fever sweat with a fleece pullover

White — my walls
my hair
my blood cells

Pink — Lyft pinging me
that my driver Mohamed
has arrived

NOTIFICATIONS

How was your first day???
from Mom at 10:02 p.m.

I type a response, delete it.
I hate my weak body, my weak mind.

I can't believe I'm already failing
at college, and it's only Day Two.

A new banner flies across my screen,
tempting me to fly out the window.

New posts from shannicollins03.
I open Instagram just to punish myself,

just to see her posing in front of a
coral-colored stucco storefront

or a dry prehistoric seabed,
saguaros fading to the blue horizon.

Tucson. Tucson of all places.
The word alone dries out my mouth.

She looks happy there.
She cut her hair, got a pixie.

She looks older, more sophisticated.
Like she's outgrown me.

BENEATH SHANNON'S POST

is an ad for an astrology graphic tee.
I half-scroll past it, then do a double take.

An uninvited guest has arrived
at this planetary dance—

Malachite boomeranging in
and out of the solar system,

a marvel of orbital gravity,
a brush so close

I feel its wind of passage
through my screen.

Unnerved, I punch *Hide Ad >*
It's Inappropriate.

There's nothing on my phone
connecting me to Malachite, so how . . . ?

Can an app know what I saw
through a telescope?

Can an app know what I half-sobbed
to Shannon last night?

I believe in strange synchronicities.
I believe that once something swims

into your awareness, you start
seeing it everywhere.

But this doesn't feel like a sign.
It feels like surveillance.

has yellow clapboard siding
and a hand-painted sign that hasn't
been touched up since the '70s.
Inside, it smells just like any co-op,
herbal and clean.

I find the lemon, honey, and cayenne,
but the echinacea eludes me.
I pace the Health & Beauty aisle,
feeling more illiterate with every pass.

"Anything I can help you find?" someone asks.
Middle-aged, olive skin, wavy black hair.
Like royalty, she has rings on every finger.

"Echinacea?" I croak. "Tincture, not tea."

"Oh, you're looking right at it," she says,
reaching past me to grab a brown glass bottle.

There's something familiar about her,
a rosewater body mist I've smelled before.

She folds my fingers around the tincture,
and when her hand touches mine,
I remember.

The sizzle of tofu fajitas,
the slant of dying light through the leaves,
the incense-blanketed darkness of the palmist's tent.

"Deva," I say.

And when she smiles,
it's so goddamn mysterious.

THE PYRAMID

"Where are you carrying the pain?"
Deva asks, and I don't know
because it's everywhere.

Eyes closed, palm extended,
she reads my energetic field.

When she opens her eyes,
they seem fuller somehow:
all my data downloaded
to her psychic storage.

"There's an imbalance," she says,
"in your root chakra,"

and she must be full of shit
because

                         that's
                   the pelvic floor,
               the chakra responsible for
             a basic sense of security. It's
         the bottom of the pyramid of needs—
       food water shelter—which means there's a
                   crack
                               in my very foundation.

THE SPHINX

At that moment, a John Denver lookalike
comes around the corner with a handful of herbal teas.
"You all finding everything okay?" he asks.

I look back at Deva, who is smiling opaquely as a sphinx.
"You don't work here?" I ask.
                                "No, I'm just nosy." She laughs.

"Here, why don't you take this as well."
She hands me a bottle with a Chinese dragon on the label.
"Wasabi will help too, but it won't go down as easily."

The price tag bumps my fever up a couple degrees.
"It's my treat," Deva says. "We can use my member discount."
Her kindness shaves the mane off my pride.

Deva pays for everything, including some wasabi and miso paste,
and makes another offer I can't refuse—a drive back to campus
in her (surprise surprise) green Subaru Outback.

"What does it mean?" I ask, clenching my teeth as I'm seized
by another shivery spasm. "The problem with my chakras.
How do I fix it?" I want to not be sick. I want to not feel

so fucking alone.
                    "Do you want to come over for a cup of tea?"
Deva asks. This sphinx riddle is easy. The answer is yes.

THERE'S AN UNBLINKING EYE

painted on Deva's front door,
its iris the same sky-blue
as the background of
the Wheel of Fortune,
the card that tells me to
bloom where I'm planted
when all I want to do
is violently uproot myself,
but maybe I can be
like the wild mint consuming
the sign in Deva's yard
that advertises her services,
maybe I can photosynthesize
this small shitty town
into pure liquid witchcraft
sweetening my bloodstream,
maybe magic is like groundwater
and Deva has tapped into
a whole fucking reservoir.

THE SHAPE OF THE SOUL

The first thing I notice are the smells
layered delicately as bible pages—
sandalwood, rosewater, orange peel,
and that nameless antique-y musk
of tarnished metals and dusty rugs.

There's mystical crap everywhere,
glass cases full of pearl-clutching dragons,
recessed floor-to-ceiling bookshelves
bursting with Ayurvedic cookbooks
and astrological ephemerides.

Without asking, Deva pours me
a cup of licorice tea. Hunched over
its sweet steam, I make eye contact
with a tiny black cat crouching
on top of the fridge, which is covered

in faded photographs of date palms
and dusty ruins and the great
Pyramid of Giza. It wears the sun
like a crown or a revelation.
I ask Deva if she's ever been.

"Lifetimes ago," she says, peeling
a postcard off the fridge. "Look.
The ancients knew the soul is shaped
like a pyramid. The stronger
our base, the longer our reach."

She looks at my brokenness
and asks me what I'm so afraid of.

I'M AFRAID

that Bailey is wrong,
that NASA is wrong,
that I was wrong
when I told Shannon
we'd keep in touch,
that the distance—
growing between
me and her,
shrinking between
Earth and Malachite—
will end us.

THE WORDS I NEED TO HEAR

Deva takes both my hands in hers
and tells me to visualize healing light
traveling up my chakras

> root, sacral, solar, heart,
> throat, third eye, crown

and to repeat after her:

> "I am, I feel, I do, I love,
> I speak, I see, I know."

A cleansing ritual, the equivalent
of an alcohol swab before a blood draw.
Now here comes the pain—

"The challenge of the highly evolved soul,"
Deva tells me, "is to speak your truth
even when others laugh and look away."

Desolation lumps in my throat
at the memory of Shannon crumpling up
her coven membership like an old receipt.

"Don't pity or scorn the less-evolved souls;
they simply haven't lived as many lives.
They don't know the things you know."

I swallow the lump, knot my fists.
I don't want to live in a world
where no one shares my beliefs.

Deva gives me a look of polished obsidian.
"Don't fear the change that Malachite brings,"
she says gently. "Even if change is painful. Our planet is sick—

it has been for a long time.
Malachite is the stone of deep healing.
It's coming to burn the sickness away."

LIKE CURES LIKE

One part beesting to nine parts sugar water:
a remedy for puncture wounds.

Diluted in the Atlantic, a drop of coffee
cures insomnia. Even after it runs clear,

water remembers that cuttlefish ink
soothes a prolapsed uterus.

Deva's homeopathy kit is just like my mom's—
red plastic with a childproof clasp.

She gives me *aurum metallicum*, essence of gold,
because the cure for sadness is beauty.

Teagan is gone, but her scent—
synthetic strawberries—clings
like Saran wrap. I spritz the air
with organic lavender mist
before collapsing into bed.

I will not be afraid. I will rise
to my purpose. I will share
my knowledge with the world.

Sleep bathes me in a tropical tide
as Deva's remedy patches the crack
in my foundation with gold.

Some
hours
later

I'm awake and sipping my tea
when Teagan returns,
Bailey right behind her.

I choke on a mouthful
of honeyed echinacea.
I'm unshowered, and
I look like shit.

"Hey, you look so much better!"
Teagan exclaims, hanging her purse
neatly on its Dorm Essentials hook.
"Did the health center help you?"

"Not remotely," I say. "Zero
out of ten stars. They're just puppets

of the pharmaceutical industry.
All they learned in med school
was how to overprescribe antibiotics.
They have no idea about herbs
and homeopathy."

"Wait," Bailey says. "You don't
actually think homeopathy works."

I bristle. "I *know* it works."

"Okay, hang on." He pulls up a video
on his phone: *Homeopathy Debunked!*
As I'm listening to the narrator
joke that if water has memory
it would remember the fish shit
and oil spills too, and that there's
no clinical evidence that homeopathy
is more than a placebo,

I'm trying, god I'm trying so hard,
to hold myself together,
but Bailey's triumphant smile
splits my gold scar open again.

SEPTEMBER

LEARNING OBJECTIVES

Biology

> We'll learn all the organelles,
> but not that a cell is microcosmic of the universe,
> that we're all part of a larger intelligence.

Algebra

> We'll learn that numbers can be negative and imaginary,
> broken and reassembled without gold to patch the cracks,
> but not that they have spiritual as well as numeric value:
> 1 for isolation, 2 for love, 3 for creativity, 4 for death.

Psychology

> We'll learn that consciousness is synonymous
> with the nervous system, that when we say
> spiritual experience, we mean a flood of chemicals.

American Lit

> We'll learn that Hester Prynne was punished
> for five minutes of pleasure with a lifetime of pain,
> that you'll live as society dictates or you'll live
> the fuck alone.

THE ART OF TEXTING YOUR BEST FRIEND
(WHO IS JUST SUPER BUSY)

9/2, 11:36 a.m. *You'll never guess who I ran into.*

9/2, 11:42 a.m. *Hey, wanna FaceTime tonight?*

9/4, 5:53 p.m. *THIS is the dining hall's sorry excuse for vegetarian. [2020904.jpg]*

9/7, 2:33 p.m. *What's your address? I want to send you a ~surprise~*

9/9, 7:07 p.m. *Fucking kill me, my roommate just said "the devil is crafty as heck." Like isn't that the only time Christians are allowed to say "hell"?*

9/12, 12:11 p.m. *Can I call you later? I'm free after 4. Are you PST or MST? Why'd you have to move to the state with the stupidest time zones lol*

9/15, 1:06 p.m. *Hey just making sure I have the right number. This is Crosby btw*

9/17/20, 9:16 a.m. *hi sorry i just have a lot going on, maybe sometime this weekend*

9/17/20, 9:17 a.m. *Hi! Yes! This weekend!!! ☺*

TODAY, 7:01 a.m. *Hey, so I guess you're still busy? No worries, I totally get it. Maybe next weekend?*

TEAGAN MUST BE A VIRGO

She makes friends easily,
a butterfly colony of choir girls
and pastors' daughters.

They leave bright slashes
of color on our floorboards
after their nail-painting nights.

They volunteer at nursing homes
and therapy horse barns
and suicide hotlines.

Not like my own hobbies
are fattening children for the oven
or sending huntsmen after hearts,

but I can't imagine raising
funds or flags or awareness
and feeling like it's anything

but performative charity.
Are they faking it,
or do I just suck?

My north node in Virgo says
you're supposed to be helping people.
Hell. These days I don't even know

how to help myself.

THE CORVALLIS-NEWPORT HIGHWAY

Teagan must've rehomed all the orphans
and outlawed all the abortions,
because she makes me her new charity case.

Which is how I find myself in the way back
of Bailey's burgundy minivan,
squished against the sticky armrest
as Teagan's friends screech along
to Disney songs I haven't heard in ten years
but still remember all the words to.

I mouth the chorus of "Just Around the Riverbend"
to myself as I watch the autumn-gilded trees
flash by, reminding myself that in forty minutes
I'll be walking barefoot on the beach.

The Corvallis-Newport Highway takes us
all the way there. Notice it's not
the *Newport-Corvallis* Highway.
The road's very name moves westward
and doesn't go back.

REFLECTION

On some unspoken signal, everyone falls silent
when "Reflection" from *Mulan* comes on,
everyone except Teagan, whose voice rises
like a harvest moon, round and clear and bright,

and for two minutes and twenty-seven seconds,
I forget that my soul is the wrong shape.

Teagan sings like Shannon glides through a floor routine,
like making a paper crane from memory,
precision in every note, every step,

and I think the universe must have a reason
for giving me people who live by Google Calendar
and wait for the oven to heat to 350°
and accept that 2 tbsp is a single serving of Nutella.

The universe has a reason for everything.

IN A GALAXY FAR, FAR AWAY

Our first stop is a counter-service Mexican place
where I try hard not to think about the quesadilla maker
I got Shannon for Christmas two years ago,
how she loved it so much that she sent me a picture
of it buckled lovingly into her passenger seat.

Bailey plops beside me with a "hey, Grandma,"
and begins devouring his chicken tacos
like his lawn Godzilla devours garden gnomes.

"Hey, Rude Grandson," I say, because I haven't
forgiven him for shitting on homeopathy.

He laughs a spray of shredded lettuce.
"Episode Five: Grandma Strikes Back."

I stab my gluey cheese enchiladas.
"Episode Two: Attack of the Crones."

He chip-dips the watery salsa.
"Episode Four: A New Hag."

Despite myself, I'm grinning around
a mouthful of microwaved rice.
"That's so stupid," I say.

"What's stupid?" Bailey's friend—
the jackass Faux-Satanist—plops down
two plates of Combo Numero Quatro.

"You," I say, unfiltered as ditch water,
and I know this isn't what Deva meant
when she said to speak my truth,
but damn—the look on his face!—
it feels good.

HEAVEN AND EARTH

It's a steep,
    zigzagging descent
        to the beach below.
            The salted wind
                combs my hair,
                    pinkens my cheeks.
                        I fill my lungs with
                            the smell of rotting kelp,
                    my ears with the cries
                of diving seabirds.
            It's only twelve miles
        to the horizon, but
      it feels like forever.
    I leave the others
and the world behind,
    tug off my boots,
      peel off my socks,
        sink my feet into
          cold brown sugar
            so flat and hard-packed
              and glossed with water
                that it reflects the sky.

IS THIS A SAGITTARIUS THING, OR IS IT JUST ME?

In the silty pink twilight, Bailey rips open
a plastic-wrapped bundle of firewood,
pyramids it around a handful of lint,
and pulls the trigger on a candlelighter.

I've always felt an affinity with fire,
how high it reaches, how hungrily it eats,
how it can glow in quiet remembrance
or burn a whole cathedral down.

Deep inside me, there's a bed of coals
dying to explode into heat and light.
In the conflagration of my own potential,
I've barely singed the kindling.

DEFINE ENERGY

With each sip of home-brewed beer—this one a carb-y chocolate
porter—
I feel more elemental, one with the earth, the waves, the wind, the
flames.

With a shiv of driftwood, I sketch symbols into the sand:
the runic alphabet Shannon and I designed in eighth grade.

By the end of the summer, we were fluent in our secret language,
leaving notes on the blackberry brambles dividing our properties.

Every time I saw a folded square of paper flutter on a thorn,
my heart would give an answering flutter.

"Is that Russian?" one of Teagan's friends asks, and the Faux-Satanist,
gesturing with his beer, says, "No, it's Hebrew."

"It's neither," I say, and explain how you can channel a rune's power
by painting it in blackberry juice on your third eye.

> "But how does
> that work?"

"Well, when you incant a spell or write a glyph, you're harnessing
its energy by giving it shape or voice—"

> "What kind of energy?
> Thermal? Kinetic?
> Electromagnetic?"

I've seen my cat prolong enough mouse deaths to know Faux-Satanist
is just batting me between his murder mittens until I tire myself out

and I don't want to give him that satisfaction,
but my tongue is stuck on a definition of energy:

(n.) the spirit-blood humming beneath the universe's starry skin,
capriciously sidestepping the laws of physics.

It can't be measured in kelvin or kilojoules, seconds or centimeters,
can't be captured on film or video. It's—

                                        "Like a prayer?"
Teagan asks, and I say, "No," and then immediately feel bad.

My amethyst is cold against my skin
while her cross glows with some inner light.

DEFINE ASTERISM

The clouds shred apart like jackfruit
to reveal a waning Scorpio moon,
a United Airlines jet stream,
and a smattering of stars.

"What's that?" people ask,
gesturing with their beers
at the clusters of lights,
and "How 'bout that one?"

Bailey tells us with saintly patience
that of the 10,000 visible stars,
only the brightest are named.
The rest are grouped into asterisms,

which sounds like a proverb
or a punctuation mark
but is just an informal pattern
"—like the Southern Cross."

I blaze to attention at the mention
of my namesake constellation,
except it's not a constellation,
and "Why the fuck not?"

Bailey explains that
its boundaries are too diffuse,
and I say, "Show me," but he can't
because it's only visible

in the Southern Hemisphere,
which makes sense,
and god I wish these people
would stop making so much sense.

AND GOD I WISH

that Malachite would hurtle
back from whence it came

and then into the heart
of a hungry, distant sun,

and maybe it's just that stars
look closer from the coast,

but Malachite's swampy halo
is spreading like infection

from a green puncture wound
that no one else sees bleeding.

KEEP OUR BEACHES CLEAN!

Around midnight, we suffocate
    the fire in its own ashes,
stash our trash in the cooler,
    and haul everything back up
the non-accessible
    stairs to the parking lot, where

fuck   *fuck*   *FUCK*

I realize that my necklace is gone.
    The cord, the stone, everything.
Panic thrashes me in its jaws
    like a dog trained to kill.
"I have to go back," I pant,
    and everyone who's not already
half-asleep in the backseat groans.
    Mr. Faux-Satanist even has
the nerve to say I can buy another,
    but Bailey says, "I'll help you look,"
because he's the boy helping granny
    cross the street, helping kitty
down from the tree, helping you
    until you owe more than you
could ever hope to pay back,
    but fuck it, I'll let him fleece me.
I know it's hopeless, though, as we
    sweep our meager phone lights
over each weathered step,
    each false glitter of simple sand,
the wind so strong, the waves so loud,
    the darkness so absolute.
We pause empty-handed
    at our blacked-out campfire,
and Bailey's face is a moon
    reflecting the light of my devastation.

"When I was three years old,"
    he says into the wind, "my family
took me to the prairie dog exhibit
    at the zoo, and as I was leaning
over the railing, I dropped
    my binky—"
                "You call it a binky?"
I ask, smirking.
    "—right into the pit," he continues,
"and one of them grabbed it
    and dragged it underground.
So whenever I lose something—"
    he gestures at the howling darkness,
"—I imagine the prairie dogs have it."
    I twist the toe of my boot
into the sand, picturing my pendant
    and Bailey's yellowed pacifier
together in a heap of treasure-trash.
    "That probably doesn't help,"
he says with a sheepish shrug.
    It does and it doesn't. It's okay
and it isn't. The emptiness
    around my throat is weightless
and it's choking me to death.

CAMPFIRE REDUX

Maybe what I thought was magical
puberty was just magical menopause.

Maybe the archetype of the ancient,
all-powerful mage is bullshit,
and like vision or memory,
magic powers diminish with age.

Maybe I'll never astral project
into the consciousness of a wolf
or blue whale, never conjure a storm
from a cloudless summer sky.

Maybe my coals are soggy at the center
and I've burned as bright as I ever will.

A FRACTURE IN THE STONE

Back in our dorm room,
as Teagan gets a perfect
eight hours of sleep,
I google you-know-what
and get 19,900,000 results.

The Wikipedia sidebar
tells me that malachite
is a *copper carbonate
hydroxide mineral*,
silky in luster,
opaque in transparency,
with a monoclinic
crystal system.

My heartbeat backfires
at the featured article—
"Is Malachite Dangerous?"

Extremely, is the answer.
Toxic if ingested, inhaled,
or absorbed through the skin,
it shellacs the lung lining,
sandpapers the alveoli raw,
leaves you heaving for breath,

and now I'm just imagining
Shannon's lungs hardening,
turning glossy and green
as algae blooms,

and I can't breathe when I realize
that my crystal encyclopedia
said that malachite has too strong
of an energetic pulse
to be everyday jewelry,
not that it's literally deadly.

A new search and a few clicks later,
I'm on *healingcrystals.com*
scrolling through malachite's uses—
protecting against radiation,
activating the heart chakra,
balancing mood swings,
healing old trauma,
and—I stifle a humorless laugh—
treating motherfucking asthma.

NOW I LAY ME DOWN TO DOOMSCROLL

1:00 a.m.
      2:00 a.m.
            3:00 a.m.

and I'm still clicking myself
deeper into this wormhole,

refining my search terms
by date, by relevance, by keywords,

tabs metastasizing
across my browser bar,

saying malachite can heal,
malachite can kill,

Malachite will miss,
Malachite will hit,

and I don't know which
mutually exclusive truth to believe

until, somewhere in the backwaters
of YouTube, I find it—

*NASA WHISTLEBLOWER
REVEALS SHOCKING TRUTH!*

His face fuzzed out,
his voice distorted

as he tells us Malachite's public-facing path
was white-lied to prevent mass panic,

as he unveils the grim reality:
Malachite's impact is inevitable

and unsurvivable.

"—but you can find the truth yourself,"
the anonymous scientist insists,
and I can. I do. I've been training
for this my entire life, lying
in a bed of bracken fern
until the forest's secrets curled
into my open ears, whispered
words of power that I transcribed
into my spellbook in Gelly Roll pen,
knowledge I was worthy to wield
while my peers got high on Sour Skittles
and Disney Channel originals.
Now, feeling like I'm walking
through standing stones
or some shimmering portal,
parting falsehoods like cobwebs,
I click the next suggested video
and fall into the orbit
of this dark new algorithm.

THE EYE OPENS

By dawn, my panic has cooled from its molten state
into a numb pane of glass.

I take a long shower, running my hands through my hair
until my fingers are webbed with white.

My head hovers above my shoulders; when my amethyst
disappeared, it took my throat with it.

I get dressed in the dark, throw on the nearest jacket,
realize it's Teagan's, wear it anyway.

Fifteen minutes later, I'm knocking on the pupil
of the eye painted on Deva's front door,

which she opens like she's been expecting me,
which maybe she has, because she doesn't flinch

when I scream, "So when you said Malachite was coming
to burn away the sickness, you meant burn away *everything*?"

She just smiles like I've solved her fucking riddle.
"Come inside," she says. "Let me make you some tea."

Deva pours the licorice tea,
opens a tin of pistachio pirouettes
even though it's barely seven in the morning.

"Our reality is 3D," she says,
and I'm thinking
width x height x breadth,

and I'm thinking *Jurassic World,*
the *Indominus rex* lunging
through the screen to bite me in half.

"We're bound," she says, "by the laws
of matter. By the limitations of mass,
of gravity." She pushes the cookie tin

and the cylinder tips, spilling tuiles
like unsharpened pencils.
"But when you look close enough,

matter is mostly empty space.
A solid surface—" she taps the table,
"—is just an illusion of consciousness."

My fury, my fear—it all slips through
the spaces between atoms. I press
my palm against the lacy tablecloth;

wouldn't be surprised if it all
disintegrated. Truth is like music,
the plucking of a perfectly tuned string.

I know it when I hear it.
Even if I can't explain.
I can't, but Deva can.

"You're waking up, Crosby," she says,
laying her cold hand on mine.
"You're awakening. And so is the earth."

Our planet is organic. Alive. Conscious.
The trees its lungs, the rivers its blood.
And we are killing it.

"But it can ascend to a different dimension,
leave its broken body for a reality
sculpted by pure consciousness."

My cheeks are wet.
Deva folds my fingers around a cookie
and when I bite into it, it turns to ash.

I see it now, what I sensed but couldn't name.
That Malachite is a mercy killing,
a bullet to the brain.

Deva asks me to close my eyes,
plant my bare feet against the floor,
and feel the earth's vibrations.

Can I feel how fast, how urgently it thrums?
How it's vibrating at a higher frequency?
Can I learn to match that frequency?

I have to.
There's no choice.
It's the only way to survive.

INSTINCT

like a newborn seeking a nipple
like a morning glory seeking the sun
like the Columbia seeking the Pacific
like migrating monarchs seeking warmth
like a hunting hound seeking a rabbit's scent
like bodies seeking each other's comfort in the dark

i seek the truth
i find my purpose

OCTOBER

You're in the library rotunda, studying for your psych midterm. There are three suggested articles on your browser's default page. Which do you click?

a. "Is My Cell Phone Making Me Sick? Flu Symptoms Linked to Radiofrequency Radiation" **(go to 1)**

b. "The Hidden Patterns in the Portland Airport's Iconic Carpet" **(go to 2)**

c. "Seitanism: The Devil-Worshipping Cult Behind the Popular Vegan Franchise" **(go to 3)**

d. None—keep studying **(go to 4)**

1) *Yes, and in fact, the library wi-fi is poisoning you as you read this. If you're experiencing any of the following—dizziness/ nausea, fever, headache, diarrhea, fatigue, low blood pressure— seek medical help immediately. (Related article: "Overdiagnosed, Overmedicated, and Getting Sicker: How Big Pharma is Profiting Off Your Illness")* **(go to e)**

2) *If you've ever had a layover at PDX, you've probably Instagrammed your feet on the famously ugly carpet. But you probably haven't noticed that the pattern repeats 666 times per 666 square feet. What does this mean for passengers?* **(go to f)**

3) *You want a side of child labor with that veggie burger? Popular restaurant chain Vegan Eden may have high standards for animal welfare, but former employees say they don't have the same stan- dards for laborers' rights.* **(go to g)**

4) *Which area of the brain is responsible for spiritual experiences?* **(go to h)**

e. Malachite's impact is inevitable **(game over)**

f. Malachite's impact is inevitable **(game over)**

g. Malachite's impact is inevitable **(game over)**

h. Let's be real. There are more important things to study.

JUDGEMENT

Today's tarot card depicts a corpse-blue family
rising from their waterborne coffins
to greet a trumpeting angel
with hair of white flames.

Cross-legged on my meditation pillow,
I measure out my breaths like cups of flour,
trying not to panic at the image of the angel
filling the sky from horizon to zenith.

From her bed, Teagan cranes her neck
for a better look. "Is that the Rapture?"

"You know tarot?" I ask, surprised.

"I know evangelicalism," she says
with a wry smile.

I admit it—I've been a bad student
of the Judeo-Christian imagery in tarot.
And I admit it—I don't *really* know
what the Rapture is or the difference
between evangelicalism and Protestantism
and Catholicism and Anglicanism.
All churches look the same to me—
ovens for broiling witches.

But Teagan isn't heaping kindling
beneath my feet. She isn't binding my wrists
to a flaming cross. She's just kneeling
beside me on the floor and touching
the angel's blood-red wings.

"I was terrified of the Rapture as a kid,"
she says. "*Terrified*. Bailey and I
would freak out if we came home from school
and our parents weren't there.
We thought they had—" she chews her lip,
searching for the right word, "—ascended
without us."

Deva's words strike me like saltwater.
How she said the earth can *ascend to a different dimension,
leave its broken body for a reality
sculpted by pure consciousness.*

I don't have to worry about spooking Teagan.
She's been preparing for the end
since the very beginning.

And so—palms clammy, voice shaking—
I tell her what Deva told me:
That when Malachite obliterates earth,
every soul vibrating at a high enough frequency
will be catapulted into a technicolor dreamscape
unbound by the laws of physics,
and everyone else will burn.

"Well, I don't think it's going to be
quite that dramatic," Teagan says
with a soft smile that tells me
she thinks I'm full of shit.

I bite my tongue, wishing I could nail it
back in its coffin.

"I don't want to scare anyone," I say,
even though I'm corpse-blue,
tossed in waves, deafened
by a celestial trumpet.
"I just want everyone to reach
their highest potential
before January third."

Malachite's date of impact.
The first month, the third day.
One plus three is four,
the number of death.

Teagan traces the tarot card's
gold-leaf border. "The world isn't
going to end on January third."

"How do you know?"

She lifts her head, her hair
haloed in autumn sunlight.
"How do *you?*" she asks.

IT'S HARD TO FOCUS

on, say, cell division or logarithmic functions,
when something much bigger than midterm grades
looms on the horizon.

It's hard to even walk
from dining hall to lecture hall without seeing
bleeding wounds everywhere—

    a frat boy laughing about a fat girl
    he slept with on a dare,

    a weary professor flicking a cigarette
    onto a lawn full of pinwheels
    spinning in remembrance
    of veterans who died by suicide—

I can hear the earth crying, trying
to wake itself from this nightmare, but then—

    a boy in a wheelchair geeking out about D&D podcasts
    with the friend pushing him across the quad,

    a barista saying to a scrape-kneed man in cycling gear,
    "Oh, the couple ahead of you paid for your drink,"

    an adoption event for dogs on the euthanasia list,

    a girl screaming "I fucking love you!" out a dorm window
    and another girl screaming back, "I fucking love *you*!"

There is beauty, there is kindness, if I care
to look for it. There is, I think,
something here worth saving.

DONNA BARTLETT

Once or twice a week, I go over to Deva's house
for spicy chai, pistachio baklava, and occult lessons—
the only class I'm not totally bombing.

She teaches me to read the knotted threads,
the blood-blotched textile of my ill-fated palms,
the tea leaves at the bottom of my cup,
the gibbous and balsamic phases of the moon.

I read and read, everything she gives me,
and some things she doesn't. I read her mail,
but only the envelopes, and only because
I'm bringing in the pile of bills on her doorstep
before the October rain turns them to mush.

She opens the door before I knock. "Crosby," she says,
never surprised to see me, never inconvenienced.

"Hey," I say. "Looks like you got a bunch of mail
for someone named . . . Donna Bartlett?
Is that your neighbor?"

There's that sphinx smile again.
"That's my legal name," she says.

I can't stifle my startled laugh. Donna Bartlett
is a church mom trying to stack non-stackable coupons
at the Yankee Candle clearance rack. Donna Bartlett
is a dentist's receptionist who never made it
to LA or New York. Donna Bartlett is a bus driver
too tired to yell at the kids in the back
who are throwing pencils at each other.

Donna Bartlett is not Deva.

I shouldn't be so surprised—
hippies outgrow their birth names
like caterpillars outgrow cocoons.
Lindas become Lavenders.
Susans become Sparrows.

But I can't imagine Deva *becoming*.
She always has been, always will be.
When I show up unannounced,
I need her to open the door.

HIGH FIVE

On Sunday I wake early to help Deva with a yard sale.
Teagan is already up, pulling a church dress over her wool
tights.

"Are you coming with me?" she asks, and my "*fuck* no"
is ten degrees too hot, scalding us both.

"Sorry." I wince. "That was a bad joke."
But it wasn't a joke—it was just mean.

Teagan gives me an uneasy smile and an "it's fine."
After she leaves, I meet my dark stare in the mirror,

take off my glasses, put them on again,
smudging but not fully erasing myself.

I shrug on a peasant dress—mauve with violet flowers,
because purple resonates at the highest frequency.

Outside there's a hush of mist, a sheen of rainwater
on the silent streets. A cold, aching beauty.

I'm close enough to smell the mint in Deva's yard
when Bailey rounds the corner of the block.

He runs at a long lope, curls pushed back
with a Beaver-orange sweatband.

"Hey, Grandma, what's up?" He jogs to a stop,
slaps his clammy palm against mine.

The sting, the sweat, the meaty smack—I feel it
because I'm still fooled by the illusion of matter,

but what if I could transcend friction?
What if I could transcend pain?

"That was sloppy," I say. "Let's try again."
Instead of focusing on his elbow,

I focus on the spaces between atoms,
the emptiness blazing with prismatic possibility,

and the next time our hands connect,
they don't.

ENDANGERED SPECIES

"Why aren't you in church?" I ask Bailey.

"Why aren't you chopping up toads
in your swamp hut?" he counters.

Point taken—don't assume things about people.

He checks something on his Apple Watch, says,
"Sorry, Grandma, gotta run. See you at bingo night!"

Idiot boy, making me smile like an idiot girl.

Bailey's nice, sure, but being nice
never saved anyone from extinction.

POSSESSION

Deva takes too long to open the door.
Just as I'm wondering if she's already ascended,
she steps onto the porch, fully clothed but naked
as a sphinx cat without her usual eyeliner.
Her hair scraggles dully down to her shoulders.
She seems confused to see me.

"Not a morning person," she says. She laughs
the blip away, then coughs phlegmily into her elbow.
I don't comment on how she was awake
that one time I showed up on her doorstep
at random-ass-o'clock.

Her cough persists, but her lids get cat-eyed
and her hair gets ponytailed, and she sets the table
with medjool dates, marcona almonds, and whole milk yogurt.
The first non-Sysco food I've tasted in days.

While I inhale fruit and nuts, Deva sticks price tags
on Turkish coffeepots and phoenix-shaped candlesticks,
Ayurvedic cookbooks and scarves stitched with tiny mirrors.
So many beautiful things—all of them worthless
in the fourth dimension.

I think about my own possessions:
my moon phase dress, my applewood wand.
My lost amulet—a lesson in letting go.

I think about the spellbook I co-authored with Shannon,
the boxes of Peace Pasta we cooked after school,
the vegan varnish we painted on each other's nails,
predawn periwinkle for her, after-dark black for me.

And I cling tight to the world,
tight enough to break it myself.

DON'T TALK ABOUT THE BUNKER

Her friend Bear shows up an hour later
to help lift the teakwood privacy screen and rustic armoire.
He remembers me, accepts me unquestioningly,
doesn't ask stupid questions like *what's your major,*
are you in a sorority, do you have a boyfriend?

He does ask if I'm still singing, which isn't that stupid,
considering how we met. "No, but my roommate
is a music minor. She's really good."

Bear nods in approval. "Tell her she's invited
to the bunker. We'll need some entertainment
while we wait for the next big bang."

Deva, setting down a stack of gold-rimmed plates,
frowns as he tells me about ley lines,
live wires of energy crisscrossing the globe,
running through ancient sites like Stonehenge,
Machu Picchu, and the Great Pyramids of Giza.

Years ago, Bear and some other disaster preparers
bought a piece of land at the nexus of two Oregon lines
and built a bunker just in case, you know,
fate pitched a rogue planet toward Earth.

Ley lines are jumper cables for the spirit,
a launchpad for spiritual transcendence.

"We have to be selective with who we invite,"
Deva says, lowering her voice. "You understand
how important this is, don't you, Crosby?"
Throat dry, I nod. I'm honored that Bear trusts me,
but more than a little hurt that Deva didn't tell me first.

HOW

These days, my phone stays off except for emergencies,
but I risk some radiation to FaceTime my parents.

My dad picks up on the last ring,
wearing an empty chip bag
like a Cossack hat—

one of his many stupid traditions,
like addressing me as any musician
but my namesake.

"What's up, Jerry Garcia?" he asks,
peace-signing me, and how—*how*—
can I tell this beautifully oblivious man
that his daughter is doing frankly terrible.

How can I tell him as he walks me down the aisle
of his organic garden, introducing me to each leaf
of rainbow chard, purple carrots, blue dream cannabis—

how can I tell him that in a few short weeks,
everything he loves will be ash?

HERE'S HOW

I don't.

TRICKERY

There are two to six lunar eclipses a year,
which is about how often Shannon posts something.

Tonight, the full blood moon aligns
with the notification's red bubble.

It's a video, a shaky 30-second recording
of her doing an aerial cartwheel.

I watch without seeing. I've seen
this trick a hundred thousand times.

All I'm thinking about
is who's behind the camera.

REVOLUTION

Pluto completes its orbit once every 248 years,
which is about how often *I* post something,

but if ever there was a time to break hiatus,
it's now. *Speak your truth*, Deva said.

I change my profile banner to a map
of Malachite's collision course.

I post an article, a video, a wake-up call.
And I wait to see who opens their eyes.

Hey, just watched your video!
You look great. Good job
not breaking your neck.
How are you?

A row of heart-stopping, undulating dots, and then

good. super busy. you?

A firework goes off in my chest.
I almost choke on the smoke.

I just learned something really important.

that's kind of the point of college

Her humor is bone-dry and familiar.

You know those earrings you bought
at Sunspirit? The malachite ones?
I knew there was something wrong
with them.

oh boy

I grimace, push forward nonetheless.

You're really psychic. On some level
you knew about Malachite.

the planet?
YES, what do you know about it???

um, it's supposed to get really close
to Venus in a couple months.
the astronomy department
is kind of freaking out about it

"Close to Venus?" That's what they're saying?

crosby

The astronomy department is under NASA's thumb
and NASA is a government organization
and the government's top priority
isn't INFORMING us, it's CONTROLLING us

. . .
ok

I DON'T TELL SHANNON

about the bunker. Not yet.
The whole truth is too big
for her to swallow, so
I drop breadcrumbs instead.
I know eventually
I can get her to bite.

HOW TO VIBRATE AT A HIGHER FREQUENCY

1) Be grateful
a. that after twenty years, your parents still drink genmaicha tea together every morning
b. for the whoosh sound an email makes when it sends
c. because while you sneer at the salad bar's wilted iceberg lettuce, millions of people go hungry

2) Visualize someone you love
a. their auburn hair before they cut it
b. their blue eyes flecked with gold, like the ceiling of Sainte-Chapelle
c. their breathing steady as you lower the ice cube and push the needle through their earlobe
d. how completely they trust you to penetrate them with beauty

3) Give
a. tarot readings to the girls in your dorm (then cleanse your deck with lavender mist)
b. compliments on metallic eyeshadow (even though it was probably tested on rats)
c. a little more effort in your coursework
d. advice about vibrating at a higher frequency

4) Breathe mindfully
a. even when Shannon posts a picture of her new boyfriend

5) Forgive
a. Shannon for moving to Arizona and taking a bleeding piece of you with her
b. Teagan for her blind worship of a false god
c. Bailey for his blind worship of mainstream science
d. Faux-Satanist for being such a fucking dickweasel

6) Purify your diet
a. with prana-rich foods like miso, dulse, dark leafy greens
b. and remember "organic always, local when possible, dining hall never"
c. by leaving the room when Teagan microwaves her Kraft mac & cheese cups

7) Think positive thoughts
a. ?
b. ?
c. ?

FOR MY PSYCH MIDTERM

I write about the illusion of consciousness,
and when I get my paper back,
it's covered in red, the color that vibrates
at the lowest frequency.

"Let's talk," my professor says,
"about finding credible sources."

JEALOUSY IS A LOW-VIBRATION EMOTION

"Have you ever dated anyone?" I ask Teagan
as I internet-stalk Shannon's boyfriend.

He's kind of cute, I guess, his smile bright
against his warm brown complexion.
But his name—Raphael Valentine—
is some heartthrob bullshit.

Pisces rising, I think. High emotional intelligence,
low survival instincts. A wearisome romantic
shyly handing her a rose bouquet after her competition.

Teagan folds a pair of modest floral panties,
stacks them in her clean laundry pile.

I'd wager my favorite agate geode that I'm
the only person who's seen those underwear,

so it surprises me when she says, "Yeah,
I had a boyfriend in high school."

"Why did you break up?"

"You know," she says, "most people
ask how we met."

Chagrined, I refocus
on a picture of Shannon and her Pisces
overlooking a cactus-studded wasteland.

"I always start at the end," I say.

reflects the question back at me,
and the answer is an easy no.

None of the Lorane boys ever interested me,
not even Matt with his kind eyes and swoopy hair.

I saw them as a lower life-form, a standard
Shannon and I had to hold ourselves above.

While they played Halo with Cheeto-dusted fingers,
we skinny-dipped in Shannon's turtle pond.

While they peppered their backyard trees with paintballs,
we strung cedar boughs with flower chains for fairies.

Shannon always went for the low-hanging branches,
her gifts within easy reach of anyone who walked by.

STUDY MUSIC

While Teagan responds to fictional scenarios
for her public health class

and I respond to NASA's brainwashed tweets
about Malachite's close pass with Venus,

we listen to music.

We have the same guilty pleasure taste
in boy bands, radio singles, and '80s jams,

the same burden to bear when our neighbor
tells us we're being too loud,

Teagan soprano'ing *turn around, bright eyes,*
and me belting *every now and then I fall apart.*

We kill the volume when Spotify starts playing
an ad for the local fertility clinic,

and Teagan asks how my essay is going.
I glance at the swarm of angry comments—

*stupid bitch, i hope you develop an eating disorder
and die, too bad your mom didn't know about birth control*—

and remind myself there's no honey without bees.
"I think," I say, "I'm really nailing my counterargument."

A STITCH IN TIME

Surround yourself with beauty—
an easy way to increase your frequency.
Easy because Corvallis, I grudgingly admit,
is beautiful in the fall, with its golden corridors,
its mellow mists, its parhelion-streaked skies.

I go for long and longer walks each day,
past the dairy farm, past the town limits,
past the edge of the earth if I could.
I can't outwalk my own body,
but maybe I can outrun it.

My first try, I barely reach
the covered bridge behind the ag school.
But the threadbare feeling in my lungs
encourages me—I'm coming unraveled.
My second try, I cross the bridge.

My third try, a stitch in my side
won't pull loose. I want to scream,
to unspool. I want to die when I see
Bailey loping toward me,
same dumb grin, same dumb sweatband.

I brace myself for *where's your walker?*
but all he says as he glides past is
"remember to breathe," and then he's gone,
and I am breathing, and the stitch—
god*damn* him—unravels.

ASTRONOMY FOR NARCISSISTS

On some unspoken agreement,
      Bailey and I start running together.

Every Monday-Wednesday-Friday
      we meet at the covered bridge,
jog down the hazelwood path
      to Fifty-Third and Walnut, then up
Witham Hill and through
      the still-sleeping suburbs
back to campus and sometimes
      to the coffee shop with dogshit espresso
but actually good scones,
      and crumb by drop by chocolate chip,
I learn more about him.

He's training for a marathon
      because he believes there'll be
an Earth left to run on next summer.
      His favorite movie is *Contact*,
and he would literally die
      if he met Jodie Foster.
He thinks a hot dog is a taco unless
      the bun splits along the seam,
in which case it becomes a sandwich.

He calls astrology
      astronomy for narcissists.
He calls church a bad habit.

He would think I'm so silly
      for my doomsday clock,
for staying up till two in the morning researching
      Elon Musk's getaway shuttle.
Only twelve credits away from his degree,
      he thinks he knows everything.
Once I have enough evidence,
      I can save him from himself.

SAMHAIN

I clear the unread textbooks off my nightstand
and replace them with a shrine
to the dead and the dying
of the light.

I weave wildflower wreaths till my fingers bleed,
bless each acorn and barberry,
bleach a forest-found rabbit skull
in Teagan's OxiClean.

At night I light the candles and think of Persephone
descending the long spiral staircase
to the underworld, pomegranate-
red dress spilling behind her.

And I think of her waiting for the first birdsong
to filter through the ice, waiting
for a blush of warmth, for a spring
that will never come.

SHOULD I GO TO BAILEY'S HALLOWEEN PARTY?

Pros:
1) I like Halloween
2) I like parties
3) Bailey and Teagan are my friends, or whatever
4) Mulled cider—enough said

Cons:
1) I have an essay on *The Crucible* due tomorrow, and I haven't even bought the book
2) Faux-Satanist and his general jackassery
3) Every time I hang out with these people, I make a fool of myself

No, I shouldn't go.

But the cider tho.

POWERLESS

"I'm surprised you celebrate Halloween,"
I admit to Teagan as we walk to Bailey's.

Close to campus, the night is raucous
with the warm, slurred shouts of Greek-lifers
in tiresome costumes, enough French maids
to dust Versailles clean in ten minutes flat.

Modest as always, Teagan wears a gray beehive wig,
a dumpy thrifted dress, and tortoiseshell glasses
with the lenses punched out. She asked my permission
to play Grandma tonight. Permission gladly granted.

"Depends on how you celebrate," she says,
and I wonder if she's thinking of my rabbit skull.
"Like, yeah, don't actually worship the devil.
But costumes can be a way of mocking evil forces
and declaring that they have no power over you."

I'm glad she didn't say something stupid like
the darkest shadows remind us to walk in Christ's light.
She talks that way around her Bible study friends
but is more respectful of me than I probably deserve.

And as we trade the zombiepocalypse of campus
for the soft jack-o-lantern glow of the side streets,
as we walk brazenly beneath Malachite's green glare,
her words resonate beneath my breastbone.

You have no power over me, Malachite.
When you're nothing but space dust,
I'll be vibing in another dimension.
What do you think of that?

The rogue planet does not respond.

PARTY IN FIVE ACTS

I.

"Oh, I get it, you're Crosby!" Bailey crows with delight
when Teagan crosses the threshold. "And you are . . . ?"

My earrings, halved pomegranates twinkling with bead seeds,
wink the answer at him, and his eyes skim from my berry crown
to the bloody jewels at my throat to the wine-dark dip of my neckline.

"Persephone," I say, thinking it would be obvious as a partner costume,
but if Shannon were here, *she'd* be Persephone and I would be Hades,
her dark king, escorting her back to her empty throne.

"Oh, huh, not familiar," Bailey says. "Is that from an anime?"

"Aren't you supposed to be smart?"

He grins at me, gestures kitchenwards with his uninspired pirate hook.
"Aren't you supposed to be chopping vegetables?"

II.

By eight o'clock, the house is filled with the cinnamon simmer
of hot apple cider, which I wish I could spike with Wild Turkey,
but alcohol is low prana, and I can't afford to lower my vibrations.

Meanwhile everyone else gets trashed, most notably Faux-Satanist,
who has made the tasteful decision to dress as a creepy priest,
too-short robe, starched white collar that I wish would strangle him,
grabby hands jokingly groping at breasts and crotches.

Teagan and I find solace in the guac, and when the jalapeño
makes my nose start dripping and she hands me a Kleenex
from her purse, so effortlessly good and kind, I know
there's at least one person here I don't have to save.

III.

"Dude, seriously, stop," someone says after Faux-Satanist's groping
makes them spill cider on the couch. "You've terrorized everyone here."

"Not *everyone*." Faux-Satanist smirks, his beady eyes meeting mine.
"Some people are too old for me."

"Go fuck yourself, you fucking perv," I say, and I don't know where
I stand
with the universe now, because hate is low-vibe but truth is high-vibe,
so hopefully it all cancels out.

"What's wrong, you jealous?" he asks. "I can do you too,
I just need a few more drinks first." He spews a laugh,

and I am gone, storming toward the half bath
where I can seethe in peace, except it's already occupied—

IV.

—by two boys twined
around each other,
one with a sandy side-shave,
the other with mussed dark curls,
Bailey pressed against the towel rack
and moaning into the blond
boy's mouth,
then pushing him away
when he sees me
and I reflexively turn
off the light
to give them privacy
to let them reign over
the sweet-tart-
tugging hunger
of their own
underworld.

V.

The evening ends around a bonfire.

Bailey's chin is raw from beard-burn,
but he's grinning like an idiot,
his arm draped over the blond's shoulder.

Teagan, always in bed by 10:30 p.m.,
wilts into a quilt as midnight ticks by.

Back on the couch, Faux-Satanist
sleeps off his debauchery.

Curled on an Adirondack chair,
I congratulate myself for not
ruining anyone's night,

but then a familiar green light
clears the treetops, and Bailey
jibbers about the best time
and place to view it—

early January,
Flagstaff, Arizona—

and I can't help it.
I can't carry the truth myself.
I clear my throat, open my mouth.
I take this nice night in my hands,
and I fucking ruin it.

NOVEMBER

NOT THE CRAB

Deva talks a lot about past lives
and planetary alignments
but never about herself.

I know she was born in Spokane
and went to Portland Psychic School
and has a cat named Bisou.

I don't know if she was ever married
or if she has kids, and if not,
if she wanted to.

I don't know how she can be so calm
when she tells me
she has cancer.

UNTREATMENT PLAN

No—she hasn't seen a doctor.
No—she isn't going to.
No—it doesn't matter,
        because none of us
        will survive the winter.

I'M THINKING

about the sun on the back of Shannon's neck,
the whiter-white of vertebrae beneath her skin.

That inside every living person is a skeleton.
That death is not something that comes for us

but from us.

TURKEY TAIL

The bottoms have rotted out
of the decorative gourds,
and the corkboard decals
in the dorm lobby have gone
from ghosts to *Gobble Gobble!*
which reminds me of turkey tail
mushrooms fanning out from
the crevices of fallen trees
in the woods where my mom
gives medicinal herb tours,
stroking the rippled caps
and explaining how they
promote healthy gut bacteria,
boost the immune system,
inhibit growth of cancer cells,
and that's why I'm out here
in Avery Park, rummaging
through the falling twilight
for a fungus so fucking common
it should be growing
right out of my skin,
but my hands are as empty
as the suburban forest's,
the seam between soil and cement
a mouth that won't speak to me.

FIELD TRIP TO THE BUNKER

Bear's blue pickup clatters down the backroads to Beaverton,
the cabin filled with the coyote howls and gourd rattles
of his Pueblo ceremonial music CDs.

A dream catcher dances beneath the rearview mirror,
crystal beads scattering prismatic light
across the herd of turquoise buffalo
glued to the dashboard.

Bear's throat bobs as he belts *heyaaas*,
but he's not fooling anyone—he's as white
as a California license plate.

I hunch uncomfortably on the cupholder
between him and Deva, my head nearly scraping
the ceiling's sagging upholstery.

I know what the girls in my women's studies seminar
would think, know that they'd point accusatory acrylics
and hiss *appropriation*, and then, shielded in virtue,
don their blaccents and Coachella headdresses.

Is that any worse than how my mom greets people
with *namaste*? Any worse than the Buddhas
in her meditation studio or the Tibetan chuba
she wears in the winter?

What about her Ayurvedic kitcharis and chutneys,
her lotus root teas and plum flower pills,
her daughter whose middle name is Dharma?

What about Donna Bartlett from Spokane, Washington,
telling fortunes as Deva Revathi?

Bear thumps the steering wheel like an elk hide drum.
Deva melts a black licorice lozenge on her tongue.
The turquoise buffalo give me obsidian glares
as I drink my gingerberry kombucha.

I can see why Deva is so tired of the third dimension.
Looking around me, I get the feeling that none of this
is real, or meaningful, or really ours.

ONE LOVE

Crunching to a gravelly stop in Bear's driveway,
I realize why his mustache quirks upward
when he says *bunker*.

There's no reinforced concrete warren,
no vault of canned beans and soups,

just an open-air mandala
made of colored pebbles,
as wide across as a swimming pool.

Not a bunker, but a launchpad.
A portal. A nerve ending at the nexus
of two white-hot ley lines.

But it kind of just looks like
some old guy's weird rock garden.

"Go ahead," Bear says, and gestures
for me to walk across it.

My boots sink into red, orange, yellow,
moving in ascending order through the chakras,
all the way to the mandala's violet heart

where Bear instructs me to kneel
and touch the ground.

I cry out when skin meets stone.
Mid-November, my breath a visible shiver,
my Patagonia jacket beaded with cold mist,

and the ground is *hot*.
Hot like life, like a bloodstream
simmering with cinnamon and cloves,

hot like it could steam the luckless lines
right off my palm.

I look up and Bear is smiling,
shoulder-to-shoulder with Deva,
and it makes me so happy-sad

to see them growing close
as two intertwined carrots,
to feel my roots groping

at the emptiness where
my seeds aren't sprouting.

Later, beneath the prayer flags
on Bear's back porch, over bowls
of green curry and brown rice,

I ask what happens
if his loved ones don't want
to come to the bunker,

and he says everyone
is his loved one
because there is only one love,

not romantic, not platonic,
not familial, and I'll find peace
when I transcend those labels.

I think of Shannon,
and my palms burn once more.
And I know I will never know peace.

SLAUGHTERHOUSE

Shannon's tagged in a photo of a 2:35 a.m.
Denny's run, her eyes un-pupiled in the flash, her plate heaped
with some Grand Slam bullshit, ham and bacon
and Hearty Breakfast Sausage. There are so many
ways to kill a pig, including but not limited to
total planetary obliteration.
                            I wonder if Shannon
is drunk, but of course she is because sober people
don't go to Denny's after midnight. Sober people
don't let their friends' souls walk up the ramp
into the slaughterhouse. No one will put a bolt gun
between her eyes. No one will pull the trigger.
Not if I can help it.
                        And I can. I can help
by texting her *hey, when's your flight? Maybe I*
can meet you at the airport, but at the end
of the three "Shannon is typing" dots
is *sorry i should have told you earlier but*
i'm actually going to do friendsgiving here
and then, as an afterthought, *tell your family*
i say hi. No *i'll miss you*. No *i'll see you*
at christmas. Just the silence between my brain
and the bullet
               after Shannon pulls the trigger.

LEFT ON READ

I scroll listlessly through selfies, videos, unfunny memes,
people I don't know doing things I don't care about

until I land on a familiar face. Aaron Collins,
brother of Shannon, accomplisher of nothing,

has posted yet another video of himself
making stoner delicacies such as a Kraft single
melted into a spicy chicken ramen cup.

Shannon always said how lucky I was
to be an only child. No one fingering your things,
using all the hot water, leaving licked-clean
cookies in the Oreo package,

no one getting away with everything
because your parents are never there,
even when they're at home.

Does Shannon's family know
she's staying in Arizona?
Do they care?

Hey, I message Aaron.
Have you talked to Shannon?

His icon appears beneath the message.
He starts typing something,
then stops.

I throw a row of question marks into the chat.
No response.

He's probably just too high to text,
but his silence haunts me.

That night, I dream that I return home to Lorane,
and where Shannon's house once stood,
there is nothing but empty empty empty.

TODAY IN THE NEWS

a flight out of Sea-Tac went down
with a Malachite truther on board.

A scientist stripped of their laurels
and their life.

"A tragic accident,"
the newscasters call it. I call it

a warning. Someone wants us
dead.

Something is trying
to claw up my throat.

I cough
salad bar and stomach acid

into the toilet.
Flush. Re-strategize.

Clear my search history,
switch browsers, scramble my IP,

scroll the dark web in dark mode,
find the truth hiding

in shit-grade imageboards,
uncensored updates

of Malachite's collision course,
cryptic hints about the coordinates

of privately funded spacecraft,
plans to raid SpaceX,

midnight confessions
of defamed astronomers

with nothing left
to lose.

FOXHUNT

Samantha Byers, someone I went to school with,
posts a picture of Malachite's supposed trajectory—

conveniently missing the outer planets' orbits
as it billiard-balls past Venus
and back into deep space—

overlaid with an *I BELIEVE SCIENCE* filter.

And fuck, I'm so fucking tired, but I can't give up
on humanity, so I say: *It's easier to believe
an easy lie than a difficult truth.*

                                    lol what, she replies.

So tired, so fucking tired of repeating myself:
*The world governments and mass media outlets
have colluded to keep Malachite's collision course
a secret, but several credible sources
have leaked that Malachite will hit on Jan 3.*

They're on me like foxhounds,
her friends and their friends and their friends' friends,
ripping my foxfur belly open with their comments.

But worse than the mansplaining,
worse than the equations "proving"
that if you divide the number of rogue planets
by the volume of the galaxy, you'll get
a negligible chance of death-by-collision,
worse than the trolls going *stupid bitch,*

is Samantha's offhand
*wow i can't believe
i used to think u were smart
[laughing-crying emoji]*

I can handle strangers telling me
to fuck myself and puke myself
to death and rip my uterus out
so I can't reproduce,

but Samantha—we survived AP World History together.
I defended you when someone accused you
of drawing on the whiteboard in Sharpie.
You passed me a tampon under the stall door
when you heard me mutter, "Shit."

It's different when it's someone you know,
someone you exchanged mandatory valentines with
in second grade—*Happy Together. Now and Forever.*

It's different when you feel so close
to the people pushing you away.

IMPORTANT, PLEASE READ

Another day, another email from the health center
telling me my vaccination records are incomplete—
well joke's on them, I never got my shots
because that shit is full of mercury and formaldehyde,
and if they think this is an *URGENT NOTICE*,
they're clearly not paying attention
to the fucking cataclysm hurtling toward us
at a hundred thousand miles an hour.

And you know who else has screwy priorities?
My so-called academic advisor, emailing me
to say that I'm in danger of failing three classes
(like I don't already know that) and am I okay
and can I come to her office hours to discuss?
Am I *okay*? If only she could see me now.

THIS IS WHAT NOT-OKAY LOOKS LIKE

In biology I learn that blobfish
look like normal puffer fish
in their natural deep-ocean habitat,
but suffer severe tissue damage
from sudden changes in pressure
when they're pulled to the surface.

Mid-lecture, I sneak to the bathroom,
lock myself in the stall farthest from the door

and cry.

IF NOTHING ELSE

I'm getting stronger.
In lieu of English class,
I run five miles
in a cold, misting rain,
following a golden thread
of hope—winter break
is only four weeks away.
Shannon, Shannon, Shannon.
I run to the rhythm
of her name—
until new footsteps
disrupt the rhythm,
and Bailey is overtaking me,
and my mouth waters
at the unbidden memory
of walking in on him,
not because I want him,
but because I haven't
been touched in months,
because I ache when I brush
against strangers in the dining hall
or watch the stupidly wholesome way
Teagan and her friends
hold hands on their way to class,
because I can't be like Deva,
austere as ice, no attachments,
not even to her own body,
because I'm getting stronger
but I'm still so fucking tired,
so fucking heavy, and when
the weight of myself
becomes too much to carry
I wish there was someone
to share the burden.

WHAT YOU WANT TO HEAR

I collapse on the front steps of our favorite coffee shop,
gasping, almost crying for breath. Bailey disappears
and returns a couple minutes later with two scones
and two coffees, mine—god bless him—with soy milk.

"So we never really got a chance to debrief," he says,
and I fill my mouth with carbs so I don't have to answer
when he asks why I believe this particular scientist
over all the others who say we're perfectly safe.

"Are you sure," he hedges, "that you're not just
hearing what you want to hear?"

"I don't *want* to hear that everyone I love will die,"
I say with an aghast spray of crumbs.

"Okay, fine," Bailey says, "let's say Malachite
is on a collision course with Earth. You want
there to be a meaning behind that, right?
Like some kind of biblical punishment?"

"No," I say, withering at the comparison.
"This isn't, like, some desperate quest
for meaning. This is just synthesizing evidence."

"Evidence like Elon Musk's 'getaway shuttle'?" he asks.
"Where would he even go?"

I grit my teeth. "The International Space Station."

"Okay, but why? A collision of that magnitude
wouldn't just destroy Earth; it would destroy
the space station too. So we can debunk that theory.
What else do you have?"

"You know," I say, smushing my scone into oblivion,
"I feel bad for Teagan because she believes in God.
But I feel worse for you. Because you don't believe in anything."

Face hot with tears, I disappear from him,
his words plucking notes of doubt
and terrible, impossible hope
from my heartstrings.

SOMETIMES DEVA REPEATS HERSELF

I don't know how many times she's told me
that morning is the best time to read your palms
or that she eats a blob of wasabi
when she feels a cold coming on,
but I know exactly how many times
she told me to take her books,
however many I wanted,
and then grabbed my wrist
as I was stacking *Venus in Transit*
on top of *The Awakened Mind*
and hissed that I was taking advantage of her
and just wanted her stuff after she died—

just once.

RIDDLE: WHAT DO CROSBY AND MALACHITE HAVE IN COMMON?

There's some high-res bullshit of Malachite going around,
everyone calling it *stunning majestic dramatic*
like it's a fucking indie film.

It sucks everyone into its dark-green gravity,
even my parents, who don't know how to copy-paste
but somehow manage to repost the photo and tag me.

It's a free spirit like you! they say.

And my screen dissolves into warm tears
as I picture them sipping their morning tea
right up to the moment of impact.

I know that some rogue planets were ejected
from their old solar systems, and some
have always been unbound.

I know that some astronomers call them *nomads*
and some call them
orphans.

THANKS FOR NOTHING

Bailey and Teagan go home for Thanksgiving,
and I go to the Greyhound station on Sixth street.

My parents' junker Volvo broke down again,
and I have to find my own way home.

It's a dismally chilly mile from dorm to downtown,
my footsteps the only sound on the predawn street,

the solid smack of stacked heel against concrete
when all I want is to move as silently, as nothingly

as a moonbeam or forgotten dream. Deva tells me
to be in my body, in the present moment, but also

that time and matter are illusory, and I don't know
whether to become more or less of myself.

I can tell from how the Greyhound attendant looks
at me that I'm too much, too Halloween,

too bitchy to *give me a smile, sweetheart*
when he hands me my ticket. I try to love him

the way Bear would, try to see beauty
in the stick-and-poke crucifix on his neck,

but I know that by the time Malachite hits,
I'll have already forgotten him.

EVERY HOUR IS UNGODLY WHEN YOU'RE AN ATHEIST

The night bus takes me as far as Drain,
and from there I Lyft expensively
to my parents' mossy cottage
off the coastal highway.

Five in the morning and the world is musky blueberry,
everything glazed in a damp deepwoods hush;
every woodpecker echo, every rustling fern
sings to me *welcome home*.

I fill my lungs with fog as I walk
down the mulched redwood driveway,
dragging a backpack that smells
like sanitizer and Teagan's perfume.

In the kitchen window, my mom's silhouette
drinks chai beneath her hanging spider plants.
I haven't even said hello, and I'm already
dreading when I have to say goodbye.

The nightbirds are turning to daybirds.
The lights are turning on.
Each moment, as it happens,
is already gone.

HOME

is where sage sticks smoke out the bad spirits,
where my mom hands me a mug of genmaicha,
and my dad passes me the bong.
Home is petal-yellow walls and turmeric-stained soup spoons,
a shungite pyramid dampening the router's electromagnetic
fields.
Home is jade plants and Himalayan salt lamps,
singing bowls and lucky cats, everything in perfect harmony
with the cardinal directions and five elements.
Home is muscle memory—the spice cabinet, the silverware
drawer,
the pitcher of moon-infused water.
Home is the chairs we painted blue one summer, the table
looking out on the chicken coop and vegetable garden.
Home is a fever breaking on the couch,
a spine realigning, a swelling subsiding
when the body finally feels safe enough to sleep.

CLEAN CUT

When I wake, the light has gone
from yellowy to clear, like an egg
uncooking itself. My wet lashes
have painted mascara on my arm—
I don't remember what dream
made me cry in my sleep.

"She's awake! Quick, hide the drugs!"
my dad yells from the kitchen.

Judging by the sizzle of onions,
the redolence of rosemary and sage,
Thanksgiving dinner is underway
without me. With a grief punch
to the gut, I roll off the couch.
I've already missed too much time.

"You're not getting enough sleep,"
my mom disapproves. "Remember,
vata-pittas need at least seven hours.
And you should be taking half-hour
naps after lunch too. You can adjust
your class schedule around that, right?"

Compare this with that health center quack
who thought she knew what I needed
but didn't even know my Ayurvedic dosha.
No one on campus knows anything.

"Right," I say, even though I swear
I'm not going back. There's nothing
for me at Oregon State University,
nothing my professors can teach me
that will be useful in the next dimension.

"Good," Mom says as she crumbles
tofu for the tofurkey. "Your health
is the most important thing."

She's wrong about that, but I let her
be wrong. I roll up my sleeves
and grab the cedar-handled knife,
start cutting the carrots into coins.
I relax into the rhythmic *thunk*
of metal on wood. After months
of feeling a blade against my throat,
it's good to be the one holding the knife.

That is, until Mom asks, "so how
is Shannon doing?" and the next thing
the knife cuts is not a carrot.

"We haven't actually been talking much,"
I say as Mom daubs calendula cream on my cut
and taps out five homeopathic arnica pellets.

She frowns. "What's wrong? Are you fighting?"

"No, it's nothing like that.
She's just really busy," I say,
the lie thickening like vomit on my tongue.
"And she has a boyfriend now."

While Dad hollows out the tofurkey
and stuffs its cold white guts with bread,
Mom makes me Instagram-stalk Raphael
so she can analyze his physiognomy.

"He's cute!" she coos, and a phantasmal knife
reopens my cut—isn't she supposed to
be on my side? "He has a generous mouth.
And those dimples! But that means his luck
will run out in old age."

I shouldn't have mentioned him.
I don't need to hear that his high forehead
is a "prosperity mountain" blessed by heaven,
or that his philtrum is a phoenix pearl
that will grant him abundant wealth and charisma.

I scroll past sappy bullshit like Shannon
riding Raphael piggyback on an arid mountaintop,
Arizona sky bluer than God's cornea,
or Raphael spinning Shannon around
in her filmy homecoming dress,
the same shade of lifeless blue.

I pause, though, on a picture of his mouth
popped open in faux-surprise
as wax slicks down the candles
of his October birthday cake—
not a Pisces, like I'd suspected,
but a pair of perfectly balanced scales.

I don't know what bothers me more—
that his Libra is compatible with her Gemini,

or that I was wrong.

A BLESSING AND A CURSE

This is my favorite part.

The tofurkey a golden-brown dome
on a bed of homegrown parsley,
savory steam fogging the window.

The cranberries puckered up
in their orange-peeled syrup,
as sour-sweet as love and loss.

The mushroom gravy decanted
from my grandma's wedding china,
tea roses on virginal white.

The random-ass blessing we recite
from whatever page
of Buddhist mantras we flip to.

But oh no, plot twist:

Mom reaches for the mason jars
on the windowsill, mischievous smile
on her face when she tells me

that this water is Malachite-infused,
this water that is already in my mouth,
this water that I'm spitting out

on grandma's wedding china,
my plate as round as my parents' eyes,
my heart fissuring like the tofurkey,

all the heat escaping
into the cold and inevitable
void of space.

DOOMSAY (V.) | 'do͞om,sā |

To predict disaster. To determine that the benefits of saving one's family from oblivion outweigh the consequences of disrupting a holiday get-together. To stand up and realize that Malachite [see *Malachite (planet)* for disambiguation]—now the size of a small moon—shines directly on the windowsill where your mom makes her lunar infusions. To feel its green poison corroding your veins. To feel your brain overheat as it synthesizes weeks of articles, forums, video content, nightmares. To tell your parents, who taught you everything you know, that they are wrong. To say the mainstream media is lying to them. To insist they have to look deeper. To use claim-evidence-reasoning (your Writing 111 teacher would be so proud) to explain that Elon Musk and Bill Gates and Rachel Maddow and the deep state are just trying to subdue a mass panic while they board their space shuttles to safety. To strategically admit uncertainty regarding the theory that Malachite was lured forth from deep space by powerful magnets by a group of fringe environmentalists who believe the only solution to climate change is mass extinction. To offer a solution. To point at the proverbial lifeboats. To say the door is *not* too small for both Jack and Rose. To assure your parents that they're already vibrating at a higher frequency than most, that all they have to do is commit themselves to extraplanar transcendence. To say they're welcome at Bear's ley line nexus. To remember to breathe. And then, to forget.

THINGS MY PARENTS FIND FUNNY

pretending an overgrown zucchini is a penis

jump-scaring me as I'm getting out of the shower

how a dog's jowls look like a grandma butt

vintage slang like *hootenanny* and *jiggery-pokery*

giving baristas fake names (tall soy latte for Rubba Bubba!)

farting into the phone when a solicitor calls

hemorrhoids

Jack Black

the long "oo" sound

me at my most vulnerable

MARS IN LIBRA

Mars is in its detriment here because Libra is the opposite sign to
Aries, which Mars rules; therefore, the direct action of Mars is
somewhat limited by the need for the approval and cooperation
of others.

                    —The Astrologer's Handbook

Picture this—the god of war smoldering in horned helmet
and spiked armor, losing his patience trying to balance
a brass scale, steam gushing out from his flared nostrils
as he backhands the whole contraption against the wall.
The gauntleted hands of war cannot make peace.

Now picture this—the nervous laughter
of people with harmonious Mars placements
who cannot understand your freefalling fury,
your stifled, white-hot screams. How you want to punch
a hole in the sun and eat its heart, blood incandescing down
your chin.

You're determined to have a bad time.
That's what Mrs. Collins said when you sulked
for hours after Shannon got a guinea pig
for her eighth birthday. Bad example, but whatever.
The point is, how can you unburn yourself from ashes?

If you heal too quickly, they'll doubt you were ever
in pain. If you smile, they'll doubt you were ever sad.
Maybe you don't choose the freefall, but you choose
not to break it. You want to see how sorry they'll feel
when you hit the bottom.

SUCCULENT

"Wait, stop," my mom says, snatching at my sleeve
as I storm away from dinner. "I believe you. I really do.
I just think you're funny when you're serious."

But I'm already across the hand-braided rug
and out the door, already gusting through the field
that separates my house from Shannon's,

the night purple as a broken blood vessel,
the Virgo moon like an unresponsive power button—
off, OFF, I want to turn it all off—

but the blackberry bramble remembers me,
lowers itself like a virgin-dazed unicorn
so I can cross the threshold and rake myself

past Shannon's dark window, the muddy light
from the moon and Malachite illuminating
her canopy bed, her succulents that I realize

have been fake all along, their meaty leaves
plastic-flourishing after months of neglect
while I wilt down to dust in my too-small pot,

and I guess that is how
I know I'm still alive.

HALF AND HALF

I stand brazenly before the dining room window,
but my only audience is a store-bought pumpkin pie
missing three slices. Shannon's parents always hated
cooking, their freezer a hoary vault of patriotic popsicles
and dolphin-unsafe fish sticks, their sink overflowing
with cereal bowls. They seemed to do everything halfway,
eating without cleaning, gardening without harvesting,
content to let the earth turn carrots back to compost.
I could see it in Shannon too, how she often left
a seltzer half-drunk, a movie half-watched, a promise
half-kept. Now, watery light flickers from the den,
an unsleeping TV irradiating the house with low vibrations.
And yes, good for Shannon for escaping, but I always
thought I'd be the one to break her out. I made her parents
my enemies, sketched them with cat fangs and knife fingers,
held Shannon close when they drank too much, yelled too loud.
Two fields away, a sheep baas and it sounds like a heart
breaking.
I wait and wait for someone to walk through the dining room,
to startle and drop a glass, to demand what I want from them,
but only light and canned laughter cross the threshold,
and so, like a song that doesn't know how to end,
I just fade away.

AARON

I can't go home, not yet, even though I want to
stuff myself with green beans and candied yams.

So I walk the perimeter of Shannon's property,
a palimpsest of memories, our childhood ghosts

still practicing backflips on the trampoline.
No—not ghosts. The trampoline is occupied

by a smoky silhouette, Shannon's brother Aaron
getting stoned by himself. "Oh hey, what up,"

he says, saluting me with his joint. Not surprised
to see me, but why would he be? I'm the ivy

at their border, always creeping toward the center.
They can cut me back, but not away.

"Hey," I say. "What are you doing out here?"
He shrugs. "Just chilling. Wanna come up?"

Just chilling. That's all he ever does,
chill at the river or the bowling alley

or the gas station he's worked at for five years,
selling pickled eggs and stale cigarettes

to loggers with flatbeds stacked high
with still-bleeding fir trees. "It's chill,"

he'd say, throwing in a free Bic lighter.
He was always chill with me too, letting me

use the staff bathroom or swipe expired Clif Bars
or hold the beer fridge door open on hot days.

Maybe it's the weed miasma, but I'm already
feeling more smoke, less fire, as I climb through

the mesh safety net to join him on the slackened mat.
My heart-springs stretch and coil at the memory

of sleeping out here with Shannon on summer nights,
waking in the saggy middle in a tangle of limbs.

"You see that?" Aaron asks, blowing fumes
at Malachite, green on black like mold on old coffee.

"Stupid fucking piece of shit," I say.
It feels good to trash-talk it, to clench my fist

and imagine green dust sifting between my fingers.
"Word," Aaron says.

A DIFFERENT SHANNON

"Is it weird?" I ask him.
"Not having Shannon here?"

He shrugs, scratches his neck.
"I mean, she always said
she was going to leave."

I feel like
I've been slapped.

He's talking about
a different Shannon—
he must be.

"She never said that
to me," I mutter, flushing
hot in the dark.

An ember appears
in front of me, the end
of Aaron's joint.

"Here," he says.
"Looks like you need this."

THE LAST TIME I GOT THIS HIGH

was our graduation after-party,
a June evening thick with gnats,
the riverbank churned by flip-flops,
our tongues blue from sheet cake frosting,
our sweat-stained polyester robes
flapping from the black oak branches.

I was happy then, stitched up with laughter
as I tried to explain to Samantha Byers
how the pyramids and the mammoths
existed at the same time, how time distorted
around the Hint of Lime Tostitos chip
that took me 4,500 years to eat.

But beneath the warmth was a permafrost
of guilt. Like I had cheated my way
to this high. Like I should have been able
to achieve this transcendence on my own.
What kind of witch was I if I couldn't
produce my own enchanted smoke?

A few inner tubes away, Shannon took
too big of a bong rip and vomited
Safeway-brand potato salad into the river.
My heart lurched toward her, but my legs
wouldn't move. I could only watch
as she poured herself into the water.

BAGGAGE

I tell Aaron everything
I told my parents, everything
I've been trying to tell everyone,
and his silence is like a stranger
on a plane helping lift your luggage
into the overhead compartment
that will remain closed until
you reach your final destination.

MAYBE ALL I WANTED

was for someone   to listen
and not tell me i'm wrong
i'm right   i'm cute i'm crazy
to   breathe in
what i'm   breathing out
and not question it   the way
you don't question
the air keeping you alive

"You know what's so scary about space?" Aaron asks.

It's the first thing he's said since Cleopatra died
and the last mammoth bled out on the steppes.

We're sprawled on the trampoline mat, arms crossed
sarcophagus-style on our chests, staring up at the stars.

I turn my head to look at him, am struck by how
not-Shannon he is. They share the same berry-brown hair,
but his is buzzed short. From nape to chin, a turtleneck
of acne. Nose jankily healed after a playground accident.
Beneath the fug of weed, he smells like 2-in-1 shampoo.

"What?" I mouth, suddenly too drowsy to speak.

He gestures at the sky. "It's not, like, something
the Avengers can fight. You know? Malachite
isn't piloted by aliens or whatever. It doesn't
even want to kill you. It just . . . is."

Breath floods my body. He gets it, he fucking gets it.
For months I've felt like a park ranger yelling
don't poke that bear! as they poke poke poke,
and finally—someone who knows when to run.

YES

I whisper.

The light in Aaron's eyes changes.
The bounce mat turns to tar,
flypapering me down as he

      eclipses
            collides

rolls on top of me and

     presses his crotch
            against mine

       tries to open
            my mouth with
    his tongue

I try to scream,
but there is no
sound in space.

SHIELDS DOWN, OXYGEN LEVELS LOW

"What the fuck?" I yell, finding my voice.

My rage fortifies me—I shove him off
with low-grav easiness.
The mat buckles,
trying to pull us back together, but I'm
already scrambling out the net flap,
scraping my knee on a spring as I go.

"Wait," Aaron says, crawling toward me.
"What happened? I thought you wanted—"

"Because we were having a nice conversation?
Because 'this girl is *deigning* to talk with me,
so she must want to fuck me?'"

"What? No. Shit. That's not what I—"

"You're my best friend's brother."

I sway unsteadily in the damp grass,
barefoot because I left my shoes
on the trampoline, nauseous because
that's not the clincher I thought it was.

It doesn't matter who he is—he should've asked first.
And something in his cheap whiskey eyes tells me
he knows what I know—that Shannon isn't
my best friend anymore.

"Fuck you," I say, and storm away
before he can see me cry.

PHONE A FRIEND

I fizzle to a stop
near the little yurt
where my mom
hosts drum circles
for her sacred
femininity group,
gourds and djembes
tempting me to break
open the night
with a fury of blows,
but instead something
possesses me
to text not Shannon,
not Deva, not 911,
but Teagan—

*this Thanksgiving
is CURSED—*

and almost immediately,
she writes back—

*Are you ok? Do you
want to talk?—*

and I don't, not really,
but it makes me feel
better just knowing
she would listen if I did.

PULSATILLA

I go home.
Because there's nowhere else to go.
Because I can't spend the night in the woods.
Because the property is rampant with memories,
each as rotten-sweet and secretly sharp
as blackberry brambles.

When I open the door, my mom
is waiting at the kitchen table
with her red plastic case
of homeopathic remedies.

She knows better than to touch me,
and I can see her face fighting
to stay neutral as she shakes out
five pellets of Pulsatilla.

A very good medicine for women,
according to James Tyler Kent's
1897 *Materia Medica—especially*
tearful blondes.

I make a PMS joke before Mom can,
though I haven't bled for months
and probably won't again.

My body knows the futility
of fertility, sees no point in blooming
when it cannot, will not
come to harvest.

On the table beside me, the *Materia Medica*
lies open to ancient wisdom
from the American father of homeopathy,
telling me I am

easily irritated, extremely touchy,
prone to melancholia, sadness, weeping, despair,
that I am *fanatical: full of notions and whims,*
easily led and easily persuaded.

I can practically hear Bailey
dismissing Kent's medica as the ramblings
of a sexist old motherfucker,

but maybe that's my own voice I hear.
Under my tongue, the sugar pills
turn to acid.

OKAY, TELL ME AGAIN

my mom says as I inhale
my reheated dinner.

"I promise I won't
laugh this time."

Mouth full of mushroom gravy,
I hesitate. I hesitate because

there are two ways to read
the Death card—

as a metaphor for change
or a harbinger of loss.

Loss, like what was lost
when good-vibes psychics

flipped the rhetoric and said
there are no bad cards, only

challenge cards. Said that
wildflowers grow from battlefields,

forgetting that soil can be salted,
that loss can be permanent.

Which is all to say that
my mom is the first kind

of reader and I am the second,
that even among mystics

there are different interpretations,
and in a body of knowledge

built from impressions and intuition,
it feels wrong to claim

that my interpretation
is the right one.

Even though
it is.

AND FURTHERMORE

my parents are
    high-vibe
    far out
    free love
    tuned in,

with their
    wi-fi dampeners
    energy amplifiers
    unconditional love.

They don't need me.
    I have to help
    those who do.

HALF-TRUTHS

I'm stressed about school.

I haven't been sleeping well.

Or eating enough.

I don't want you to worry.

REALIGNMENT

I wake with the dawn,
feeling like a fever
has broken. Feeling
each cell in my body
realigning to its purpose.
I have wandered off
the path, been mired
in the red wastes
of my lowest chakra,
when I should be
beaming myself through
the grimy skylight
of this doomed dimension.

From outside—the sound
of devouring. Aaron,
electric hedge trimmers
in hand, razes ivy
off the fieldstone wall
dividing our properties.

Briefly, I buckle beneath
his remembered weight
but then release him.

I thank him for teaching me
that I can drop anything
I don't want to carry.

MISSION STATEMENT

Sunday morning, my parents walk me down the driveway.
My Lyft idles by the mailbox that Shannon and I painted
with hummingbirds and sunflowers
the summer before fourth grade.

My backpack is laden with prana-rich snacks—
raw almonds, coconut date rolls, curried chickpeas—
but I barely feel the straps digging into my shoulders.

I am transcending friction. I am transcending pain.

I am light passing through a crystal,
and nothing can hurt me.

DECEMBER

TEXT TO SHANNON

<image.jpg> A rock garden in a mandala pattern

You are cordially invited to an out-of-this-world #LaunchParty

Life as we know it may be ending, but we can keep the party going in the afterlife! Join us for a ley line–charged evening of revelry and transcendence as we jumpstart our souls on their immortal journey beyond the illusion of consciousness. Good vibes only!

When: January 3, 10:00 a.m. until time becomes meaningless
Where: 1612 Old Hollow Road, Beaverton, OR
What to bring: Your open mind

See you in the fourth dimension!

BACK ON CAMPUS, BACK ON MY SHIT

At the Beaver Store, I buy five boxes of pushpins and a roll of tape.
In the Valley Library, I make 500 flyers of Malachite's path of impact.

Working my way across campus, West to East from Rabbit Research
Lab to Autzen House,
then South to North from the oceanography lab to Burt Hall,

from the fluorescent-lit garden levels to the higher floors,
I cover every corkboard and dorm room door.

The dean sends a student body–wide email saying that whoever
is propagating these harmful conspiracies needs to stop,

but what can he do to stop me? The dean couldn't suck a dick
if it hit him at sixty-seven thousand miles per hour.

SUMMER SONG

Radio pop and synthetic strawberries
greet me when I stumble into the dorm room.
Teagan mashes the mute button on her laptop,
panic flashing through her eyes like the devil
has knocked down her door.

I look the part—eyes sunken
in smudged black liner,
hair cobwebbed with split ends.
My reflection in the full-length mirror
is a haunted thing, hollow with hunger,
unrecognizable and nothing
like the cleansing violet flame
inside me. I guess enlightenment
can't substitute for a shower.

"No, it's okay," I say, and we smile
shy and doe-like as the music
refills the room like oxygen,
the kind of windows-down,
summer-synth joyride bop
that almost makes me feel
like I had something good.
Like I let it go.

ELEVATE YOUR SPACE: DORM ROOM EDITION

1) Strip your mattress and wash your bedding in organic lavender detergent

2) Wrestle your mattress to the floor and out the door as your roommate watches in confusion

3) Explain how the metal springs amplify radio waves that can cause cancer and interfere with one's spiritual frequency

4) Hear Bailey's voice in your head snickering *you know what's a more powerful source of radiation than your bed? The sun*

5) Run into your RA, a dour, pear-shaped girl who goes "stop, stop, what are you doing?" and watches, arms crossed, as you sullenly drag the mattress back onto its bolted-down frame

6) After she leaves, call Buildings & Grounds and explain that for health reasons you need to have your bed removed. Grit your teeth at their bemused questions, their suggestions that maybe you have mold or other allergens in your dorm, that you should make an appointment at the health center

7) Hang up, stare hopelessly at your shitty, radioactive bed

8) Pack a bag. You're going to stay with Deva for a while

KISS OF DEATH

Deva's Subaru is in the driveway,
but her paisley curtains are closed,
the arteries of her house silent
when I press my ear against the door.
I turn the handle, let myself in,
nearly gag on the miasma of decay.
Hold my breath, make my way
past the living room—empty—
the kitchen—empty—muffle a shriek
as something brushes my ankle.
The coarse, slinky shadow
opens its pink mouth and *meows*,
and the tension pours off my shoulders.
I scoop Bisou into my arms.
Bisou, French for *kiss*.
I press my lips between her ears.
A rusty purr starts deep in her chest—
too much rib, not enough heartbeat.
Her bowls are both empty,
her litter box overflowing.
The sink brims with sour dishwater,
the compost with rot-streaked
avocados and liquefying onions.
Together, Bisou and I push deeper
into the dark. Deva's name dies
in my throat, extinguished
by the oppressive silence.
I find her slumped in her office
chaise longue, hair grayer
at the roots than I remember,
and even though I haven't been
to a hospital since I was born,
I have the strangest impulse to call
an ambulance, to see an IV
of something stronger than turmeric
in her dehydrated veins, but no—
Deva knows better than Western doctors.

The only things waiting for her in the ER
are misdiagnoses, overprescriptions,
labyrinthine insurance paperwork,
and enough EMF waves to blind
her third eye permanently.
So instead, I go back to the kitchen.
I fill Bisou's bowls with electrolyte water
and grain-free chicken liver pâté.
I put the kettle on to boil.
I close my eyes and imagine
Deva's body bathed in golden light,
purifying, fortifying, burning away
the sickness that binds her
to this cruel, polluted dimension.
Deva said I'm an old soul.
She said I'm strong.
Strong enough to save her,
or at least take away her pain.
When the kettle starts shrieking,
Deva does too.

Bisou claws out of my grip,
leaving stinging red lines on my arms.
She skitters across the kitchen tile
to the doorway where Deva's specter
sags in relief, liver-spotted hand
clutched to her heart. "Crosby,"
she rasps. "It's just you."

But like a cloud crossing the sun,
her relief turns to muffled fire.
"What are you doing in my house?"
she asks, her own claws unsheathing.

"I was just——" I gesture helplessly
at the stove, where the kettle
still howls atop its ring of blue fire,
"——making you tea."

"I'm not an invalid," she says.
"I can take care of myself."

I back up enough to dismount
the kettle, collect my thoughts
as the spout exhales steam.
The strap of my messenger bag
reminds me why I'm here.

"I was thinking . . . hoping I could
stay with you for a while. Since campus
is like an energetic sinkhole.
And B&G wouldn't move my bed——"

Deva's stormy expression tells me
she doesn't give a fuck about my bed.
"You need to figure that out
on your own," she says, and I know
she's talking about more
than reconfiguring my dorm room.

And it's like being disowned,
like being furrowed and salted,
like a displeased god striking
an offering from my hands,
like looking down and realizing
that where my hands once were,
there's now only blood and smoke.

I RUN

I run in my stacked heels, with my messenger bag thumping against my hip.
I run without a destination.
Without pride.
I run with green fire in my mind.
I run with my north node in Virgo—*you're supposed to be helping people.*
But how can I do that if they won't accept my help?
If this is my destiny, why does everything I do feel wrong?
I run past the suburbs, past the ag school, past the covered bridge.
I run right past someone with sweaty dark curls pushed back by a Beaver-orange sweatband.
Bailey's footsteps get quieter, then louder as he doubles back.
He doesn't say a word, just keeps pace with me until I collapse.

"Do you want to talk about it?" Bailey asks.
"Or do you want to singlehandedly
destroy this delicate ecosystem?"

We're sitting in the wet grass off the running path,
Bailey's hands folded primly in his lap,
mine ripping clumps of grass from the soil.

I can't tell him about Deva—I'm not in the mood
for a lecture. Not ready to explain
the cat scratches puffing up on my arms.

"Why are you so nice to me?" I blurt.
He's not like Aaron, coiled up and waiting
to strike, so what does he want from me?

"Because I get it," Bailey says, reaching out
to stop me from uprooting some winter heather.
"Not the Malachite thing, but the conviction.

I was just like you not that long ago.
Bible camp, mission trips, praying to God
to 'save me from temptation.'"

I shake my head. We may run together,
but we're on different paths. He's not enlightened.
He just traded blind faith for blind reason.

"The world is such a fucking mess," he continues.
"Can't trust the media, can't trust big pharma,
can't trust a single word out of the president's mouth.

We're all just looking for answers, right?
And when we hear one that clicks—" he snaps
his fingers, "—boom. A silver bullet to all our problems.

Religion does that. Conspiracies do that.
They say 'you're special, you're chosen,
you're not sleepwalking like everyone else.'"

My fingers dig into the cold earth, the darkness
burrowing under my nails. We're not the same.
Bailey and I have nothing, *nothing* in common.

"And that's how they get you," he says.
"By giving you a purpose. By having
a parasitic relationship with your instinct

to help and nurture and share knowledge.
And by giving you community. That's why it's so hard
to leave. Higher benefits, higher exit cost."

The pain of packed dirt beneath my nails
has twisted into pleasure. Manacled with soil,
I don't try—don't want to try—to break free.

INVITATION

"You should come with us to Arizona," Bailey insists.
"There's one more spot in the soccer mom–mobile."
He counts on his fingers. "We've got me, Teagan,
Joshua, Sandeep, Eliza, and Ana Maria."

I've heard those names before at Bailey's house parties,
but I can't assign them to faces. Pretty sure Joshua
is Faux-Satanist, though, and I'd rather eat dining hall meatloaf
than spend three days in a car with him.

"We're leaving on New Year's Day," he says.
"You just chip in for food and gas. It'll be good
for you to see it yourself, don't you think?"
By which he means, good for me to see I'm wrong.

FINALS

American Lit

> In a 650-word email to the dean of the astronomy department, synthesize at least three multimedia sources from credible Malachite truthers to substantiate your argument that the department's academic dishonesty will have grave consequences. Be sure to cite your sources!

> For extra credit, compare and contrast passages of James Tyler Kent's *Materia Medica* to reassure yourself that homeopathy wasn't founded on sexism.

Algebra

> Solve the following word problem: If Bear's launchpad is approximately 20 ft in diameter and the average shoulder width is 14.4 inches for women and 16.1 inches for men, how many people can fit on the launchpad? Show your work!

Psychology

> Using her natal chart and Instagram account for reference, compose a 300-word discussion post analyzing how and why Shannon has become someone you hardly recognize. One letter grade will be deducted for failure to apply the stages of psychosocial development we studied this term.

Biology

> In the Health & Beauty aisle of Morning Glory Co-op, identify three to five herbal supplements that lower the risk of cancer.

> Bonus assignment (not for credit): Purchase a small bottle of rosewater body mist, douse your wrists, and breathe Deva's fading scent off your skin.

TODAY, 4:06 p.m.   *I miss you*

TODAY, 7:17 p.m.   *i miss you too*

I LOST

There's an article going around the Malachite truther boards:
"I Lost My Mom to Malachite," profiles of people whose loved
ones
have *fallen victim to the misinformation epidemic*. Eye roll.

Seaweed snack dissolving on my tongue, I scroll through
the cherry-picked quotes until one stops me dead.

> *the government's top priority*
> *isn't INFORMING us, it's CONTROLLING us*

Submitted by Nicole in Arizona. One of her best friend's ravings.
She doesn't recognize her anymore. Is afraid of her, even.
Thinks it's sad how conspiracies prey on the lonely.

The seaweed turns into the garbage-iridescence of fly wings.
Did Shannon think I wouldn't find this?
That I wouldn't recognize my own words?
Doesn't she know who made me this lonely?

MORE TOXIC THAN MALACHITE

I can't even say I'm surprised.
By your 999th cut, you know
the thousandth will kill you.
Still, it doesn't sting any less.

Alone in the dorm room,
I wallow through Shannon's
social media and then Raphael's.

He thinks he's so smart,
with his political hot takes
and his righteous infographics
and his offhand libel:

"Sure, astrophysicists have spent
their whole careers studying
planetary movements, but you
saw one Malachite meme
and suddenly you're an expert."

Fuck him. He's poisoned Shannon,
turned her against me. But I can
take comfort knowing that Shannon
alone would never betray me.

THE ANSWER TO THE RIDDLE

I'm at the co-op deli
buying kale salad and lentil soup
when a familiar voice,
wry as a squeeze of lemon, asks,
"Anything I can help you find?"

Deva, a waif in a brocaded shawl,
leans on a cane that reminds me
of the old sphinx riddle—

what walks on four legs in the morning,
two at midday, and three at night?

—and how the answer is not
some fearsome, shape-shifting beast,
but man. Mortal, breakable man.

"Crosby," she says, her voice an empty room
where anything could happen.
"I'm sorry that I hurt you."

The fluorescents glare down
on her gray roots, her paper skin.

"Last time you saw me,
I wasn't my best self."

I understand—I do. I know how pain
can turn you into the animal
the riddle pretends you are.

When we embrace, I'm afraid
I'll dust her down to nothing.

She pulls away, eyes shining.
"You were my daughter
in a past life," she says.

I WANT TO DO SOMETHING

nice for Teagan. Despite the whole God thing,
she's one of the only sane people on campus.

I don't bother with the downtown boutiques—
what good are earrings and infinity scarves
without a body to hang them on?

Instead, I break her birthday down
to its life path number—three, of course.
A human sunbeam of empathy and optimism.

Three—the number we have hypothesized
is the best track on any given album.

It isn't much, this gift, this playlist
of Track 3s, but maybe its vibrations
will harmonize with her own.

Maybe, after sound ceases to exist,
there will still be something like music.

HOME FOR THE HOLIDAYS

Before going home for Christmas,
Teagan gives me an amethyst pendant
to replace the one I lost.

As soon as I slip the crystal
over my neck, I feel less fractured,
more refracting of light.

She hugs me when I share
my dumb playlist with her.
"This is perfect," she says.
"We can listen to it on our trip."

"Are we . . . going somewhere?"

"Bailey says you might come
to Arizona with us," she says
with a hopeful smile.

I shake my head. "I have plans."

Missing Thanksgiving is one thing,
but Shannon would never miss
Christmas. I'll be waiting for her

when she pulls into her driveway.
She'll see me and shake off
the sun-stroked haze of the desert.

She'll wonder why she ever left.

AT THE END OF THE LAST SEMESTER FOR ANYONE EVER

I go home.

One more predawn walk to the Greyhound station.

One more cramped ride next to someone eating Hot Cheetos for breakfast.

One more Lyft from Drain to Lorane.

One more walk up the driveway to my parents' purple house.

One more hello before I have to start saying my goodbyes.

AT FIRST I THINK IT'S THE WINDCHIMES

but it's a text notification.
I never get those anymore.

Shannon's name lights up
my screen, my whole soul.

hey, she writes, *i'm so sorry
but i got a j-term internship*

*here in tucson and I'm going
to stay through new years*

*but i'll be home this summer,
i think, i'll let you know.*

No. No she won't.
By then, it will be too late.

THE ART OF TEXTING YOUR BEST FRIEND
(WHO JUST DROPPED A BOMB ON YOUR HEAD)

Internship? Doing what???

it's like a medical scribe thing

?? But that's not even something you care about.

i mean, it kind of is
it's good experience

You have to come home.
It's safer here.
Jan 3—can you make it?

...
i want to see you
but you know how my family is

(her mom chain-smoking on the porch,
shrieking at her dad through the screen door,
her dad slamming the fridge and yelling "if you hate me so
much, then leave!" and
the alphabet magnets unalphabetizing themselves as they fall,
Aaron pressing himself against me—)

You don't have to stay with them!
You can stay with me.

last minute tickets are too expensive

I'll pay for you.
Shannon, please.

Shannon?

Shannon?

FIRST COMES THE PANIC

blinding   suffocating   sweaty as a sleeping bag

the memory of waking up   without her

at the Sunspirit festival   how I scoured the campsite

until I found her   by a sluggish curve of the river

coloring book propped on her knees

as she turned the petals of a mandala (how is it I'm *just now*

remembering?)   lilac and rosé-pink   how young she looked

with her satin-trimmed   polka-dot pajama shorts

and her nightshirt   slipping off one shoulder

her eyelids still glittering   with yesterday's face paint

how I said   "sorry, do you want to be alone?"

how I'd   never apologized before   and it felt like weakness

how I prayed   to every pagan god who was listening

that she would say no   that she would scoot over

to make room on the riverbank   but she turned back

to her coloring and said   "yeah, sorry, just for a little while,"

a little while that will last

until the end of time

THEN COMES ACQUIESCENCE

Deva once told me that wolves will ascend
but that crocodiles will not.

Leopards but not bats.
Elephants but not ants.

Not every creature has the frequency
to make the jump.

Even among humans,
the wavelengths vary.

To let go of your ego, you must
also let go of what tethers you to Earth.

Perhaps this is my greatest test.
This letting go.

THREE WEEKS

until the green apple in the sky
ripens into a devouring fire.
Already, it's the size
of a small moon.

I spend hours a day in the woods, running
my hands through the rain-beaded sword ferns,
scraping dirt off turkey tail mushroom gills,
seeing how close I can get to a black-tailed deer
before it vanishes into the bracken.

Sometimes I walk out to the distant ridge
where the slope is buzzed as barren
as Aaron's knobby skull. It's easier
to say goodbye to the parts of the world
that are already gone.

PRAYER FOR THE WINTER SOLSTICE

May the darkest days be over.
May those who are sleeping wake up.
May Deva's suffering end.
May my father call me Neil Young or Bob Dylan one last time.
May each of my numbered mornings begin with a cup of my
mother's genmaicha tea.
May everyone I've lost, everything I've sacrificed—may it all be
worth it.

JANUARY

ON NEW YEAR'S DAY

I say goodbye to my material possessions:

A Hello Kitty notebook filled with the runes Shannon and I invented the summer before seventh grade. Margins heavily annotated with my crabbed, slanted penmanship and Shannon's ballpoint bubble letters. *For immortality. For mind control,* I wrote next to my runes. *For protection,* Shannon wrote next to hers.

An applewood bough, slender and freckled, that once served as a magic wand. Summer memories of running barefoot through the slug-strewn grass, shrieking hexes over our shoulders as Aaron barreled after us, yelling that if we ever touched his computer again—but we were too fast, his threat still hanging unfinished in the empty field.

A spiral-bound sketchbook with black pages, the kind you write on with gel pens. The poorly spelled words of an incantation to stop time. The cloudy, stratospheric elation we felt when the numbers on the microwave started blinking. Shannon and I, we were always meant to transcend time.

LET'S BE REAL

I've been preparing for this ever since
Shannon told me she was moving to Tucson.

I've always known the lengths I would go to
to get her back.

Motherfucker, I'm going to Arizona.

TRAVEL PLANS

No way am I flying—not after what happened
to the truther flying out of Sea-Tac.

My parents' '89 Volvo can't even make it
to Eugene without the engine stalling.

They look at me like I'm wearing a MAGA hat
when I ask them if I can borrow $3,000
to Lyft across the country.

I check Amtrak, check Greyhound,
find affordable tickets that will get me there
on New Year's Day. Two days before impact.

But the distance sounds so vast,
the journey so lonely.
I can't do this by myself.

Heart catching fire as it plummets
through the atmosphere, I text Bailey:
Do you still have room for one more?

THE CALL IS ANSWERED

The sound of tires on gravel summons us outside,
where a burgundy minivan is blazing down the driveway.

My parents wouldn't blink at an alien visitation,
but a van full of astrophysics grad students gives them pause.

"Think they're lost?" Mom asks, her question swallowed
by a flurry of honking. "Or here for an herb tour?"

Bailey—clad in skinny corduroys, aviator sunglasses,
and a Tootsie Pop owl t-shirt—hops from the driver's side
and throws me a sloppy salute.

"Definitely here for an herb tour," my dad says,
pretending to smoke a joint.

As Teagan and the others disembark,
Bailey strides over to squeeze me in a side hug.
"Good timing, Grandma. If you called an hour later,
we'd be in Roseburg by now."

He turns to shake my parents' hands.
"Pleasure to meet you, sir, ma'am," he says.
"I'm an upstanding young gentleman,
and I'm here to abduct your daughter."

"Thank god," my dad says. "I can't stand her."

"You didn't tell us . . . " Mom starts,
but there's too much I haven't told her.
"Where are you going?"

She side-eyes Teagan, who's wearing
a tie-dye Bible camp hoodie.

"Tucson," I say, my mouth suddenly
as dry as the dust-deviled desert.

"It's the best place to view Malachite's
closest pass to earth," Bailey chimes in.

"Shannon will be there," I blurt
before Mom can bring up my nuclear meltdown
over her Malachite-infused water.

Teagan knows very little about Shannon,
Bailey even less, but they both know
that I wouldn't put myself in Malachite's
direct trajectory without a reason.

No one here *really* knows anything,
least of all Bailey's friends hovering
awkwardly around the van.

How strange that they are here.
How strange for my best friend
to run 1,300 miles away from me
and these strangers to come when I call.

SEATING ARRANGEMENT

Bailey drives with one elbow out the window
like he's in a music video.

Teagan is carsick and gets shotgun,
music privileges, and emergency snacks.

Eliza, on the middle left, passes her a pickle jar
from the cooler and says drinking the brine
will settle her stomach.

Joshua/Faux-Satanist, on the middle right,
complains about the music, the smell of vinegar,
and how Bailey refuses to use cruise control.

Sandeep, back left, is trying to administer
a quiz called "Design a Wedding Buffet
and We'll Tell You What Sex Position You Are."

Ana Maria, middle back, Doc-Martened feet
resting on the cooler, asks my opinion
as she swipes through Tinder.

"You're not single, are you?" she asks,
a joke but not, even though she punctuates it
with "kidding," and I make yet another mistake—

thinking of what I'll miss
about the body I'm trying to escape.

SEARCH AND RESCUE

"Have to pee?" Ana Maria asks me.

I'm bouncing my leg up and down
as I research maps of Arizona ley lines.

"Just restless," I say, smiling
at a powerful spiritual nexus in Sedona,
only three hours from Tucson.

Later, I'll worry about how
to get Shannon there. I won't worry—
can't worry—if our combined voltage
will be enough to make the jump.

STATE OF GRACE

Somewhere deep
in the hushed profundity
of the NorCal redwoods
is a 50-ft-tall statue
of folk hero Paul Bunyan.
Bailey pulls over
so we can take pictures,
peruse the gift shop,
and stretch our legs.
I pace the gravel lot,
in no mood to pose
for Eliza's Snapchat story.
Teagan catches up with me
by a touristy trailhead
and asks how solstice was—
this girl who believes
quite literally that Christ
died for our sins, that I
will be divorced from God
after death—calls it *solstice*.
We have our own winter
holidays, our own names
for the apocalypse—
the Rapture, the collision,
maybe it's all the same.
She has told me that we
are not that different,
that we're both searching
for a state of grace,
and when I asked
what that meant, she said
it was difficult to explain,
and somehow that alone
made sense to me.

When we cross the city limits after dusk,
everyone but me breaks out into song—
The Lonely Island's "YOLO."

Joshua, noticing my sealed lips,
goes, "What, is this song against
your religion? Because reincarnation?"

And if I could punch through his face,
I'd punch right back to the moment
in Deva's stifling brocaded tent
when she said I was at the end
of my soul's journey.

I believed her then, just as I believed
when she said I could journey
beyond the third dimension
and luminesce there forever.

This, I cannot reconcile.
So many things can be true
but not everything at once.

"So, Crosby," Eliza ventures, and I brace myself for
do you really believe in reincarnation? Are you a Buddhist?
But what she says is, "What's your starter Pokémon?"

I laugh with dizzy relief. "If we're allowing it,
Eevee with an eventual Espeon evolution.
And if we're going classic, I guess Charmander."

"Wow," Joshua says. "*Someone's* not like other girls."

"Shut up, Joshua," Eliza says cheerfully.
"Sorry, Crosby, if I let you have an Eevee,
I have to let everyone have an Eevee.
How about you, Teagan?"

Teagan throws me a bewildered look.
"Um, I was never allowed to watch it.
Can you pick for me, Crosby?"

Despite myself, I lean into the conversation.
"You're a Chikorita. Bailey's a Squirtle."

"Oh, Bailey is *such* a fucking Squirtle." Ana Maria laughs.

Bailey grins into the rearview mirror.
"Is that the gayest one?"

"No, that's Jynx," Sandeep says. "She's a literal drag queen."

"Okay, but Clefairy?" Eliza says. "Queer icon."

Ana Maria rolls her eyes. "*Clearly* no one here
has ever looked at a Cloyster."

"The fuck?" Joshua cries after a quick image search.
"Thanks a lot, now I'll never be able to unsee it."

"Wait!" Sandeep yelps, brandishing his phone.
"We forgot about Machoke! Just *look* at this gym daddy."

"Guys, guys." Bailey raises his voice over the chaos.
"Queerness is a spectrum. We need a rating scale."

Ana Maria taps something into Google.
"There are 898 Pokémon.
This will take forever."

And because I welcome the distraction,
and because this feels like the giddy, late-night
trampoline conversations I used to have with Shannon,
I say, "gotta rank 'em all,"

and with a solemn nod, Ana Maria says,
"indeed we do," and suddenly I find it
a little easier to breathe.

NIGHT ONE

We crash in a rat-hole motel
across from a strip mall,
though *mall* is a generous term
for a Chinese restaurant,
an H&R Block, and eight
empty storefronts.

I'm sharing a room with Teagan,
Ana Maria, and Eliza.
Two queen beds, one box TV
playing *My 600-lb Life*.

I peer out the heavy curtains
at a pair of maybe-coyote eyes.
A cold wind inside me whispers
that I have to keep moving.

Twenty minutes of small talk.
Fifteen minutes of waiting
for the boys to bring
sesame chicken, pork fried rice,
and for me, miso soup.

The salt floods my tongue,
fills my stomach, threatens
to come back up when Bailey
tosses a frosty Ziploc bag
of shrooms on the bed
and says, "Dessert, anyone?"

"Dude, no," Sandeep says. "Not here."

"You have to do it outside," Ana Maria insists.

"Don't *waste* them," Joshua says. "They were expensive."

Bailey throws up his hands in defeat.
"Jeez, okay, okay. Another time, then."

Teagan says nothing, a glazed smile on her face
as she scrolls through her phone.

Bailey returns the shrooms to the cooler,
and they all smoke weed instead,
a bottle of bottom shelf gas station wine
passed around between puffs.

I focus on the cloudy dregs of my miso
and hand back whatever they hand me.
Last time I got high, it didn't end well.

I don't know what to do with my hands
or my caged-tiger mind. I didn't bring
a novel or a computer or origami paper.
Just the clothes I'm wearing now,
the spellbook with the time-freezing spell,
and the moon phase dress I wore at Sunspirit.
Arizona, while it still exists, will be hot.

After a while, Bailey and the others
stumble outside to view Malachite.
Alone, I roll over to press my face
into the cheap motel bedding.
I don't even have the energy
to shut off *My 600-lb Life*.

"She's killing herself," a woman's voice sobs.
"She's killing herself, and I don't know how to help her."

SOUTHERN CALIFORNIA

is bleak heat   sky bleached

white hot   empty lots

          bloodstreams   like jet streams

dissipate   highway straight

     no shade   low-grade

feverish dreams   of silver screens

     roadkill drying   something dying

wheezing   grating   back left tire popped

          deflating

WITH A JOLT

I'm suddenly, shatteringly awake.
I don't remember falling asleep.

Desert light razors through the window,
slicking me with sweat.

We're swerving onto the beige shoulder,
trailing the flat tire's slack skin.

"Fuck, are you fucking kidding me?"
Joshua yells. "We're in the middle
of abso-fucking-lutely nowhere."

We scramble out the sliding doors
and into the midafternoon heat.

The sky is bodiless blue,
empty except for Malachite—
swollen to the size of the moon.

I focus on the low horizon,
how it throbs like a migraine,

but Bailey draws my eye skyward
when he climbs onto the van's roof
to get a better cell signal.

Framed by the rogue planet,
he calls AAA's roadside assistance.

Stupid boy.
He's reporting the wrong disaster.

"Crosby, you'll get heat stroke!"
Bailey yells out the window.

They're all iceboxing themselves inside the minivan,
singing along to sea shanty TikToks so loudly
I can hear them from fifty feet away.

I ignore Bailey's shout, staring stubbornly
at the rippling mirages of tow trucks
as if I can will one to materialize sooner.

We're running out of time we're running
out of time we're running out of time we're—

My heart revs up as a truck approaches,
but it's just a dusty semi, its trailer
advertising The Brands You Love.

Teagan brings me a full water bottle
and some empty reassurances.
Gratefully, I accept them both.

Millennia later, with a fresh tire on the axle
and not a single unfrayed nerve in my body,
we're back on the road, all sea-shantied out
and letting Neil deGrasse Tyson's chuckle
fill the air. I'm too defeated to even mind
that this episode of the podcast is all about
Malachite truthers' viral fearmongering.

"It just sounds exhausting," Ana Maria says
at one point. "All those mental gymnastics
to find patterns in the data that don't exist."

"I kind of get it," Eliza chimes in. "If you
really believe that Malachite will hit,
that simplifies things, doesn't it?
Humankind's problems are so complicated,
but none of them matter if we're
all going to die in two days."

She's not wrong. When I think about
the mess I left in Oregon, my trainwrecked
final grades, my question mark future—

no.

Better not to think about that at all.

FUN CAR TRIP ACTIVITIES

I sleep.
I worry.
I starve
rather than partake
of Chick-fil-A.
I ignore a call
from a number with
a Portland area code.
I scroll
through Shannon's
social media,
track her plans to camp
at our same destination,
Saguaro National Park.
I draft a text.
I delete it.
I'm afraid
that if she knows
I'm coming,
she'll tell me
to turn around.

NIGHT TWO

We pull up in a sundown ghost town,
rent two rooms in an L-shaped motel
with an outdoor pool, its turquoise chlorine
the only color for miles.

"Tonight's the night," Bailey singsongs,
shaking the Ziploc of shrooms.

Teagan politely declines,
opting for a few laps in the pool
and a few episodes of trash TV.

"You're coming, right?" Ana Maria asks me,
like she's holding open a door
instead of a plastic baggie.

"Don't peer pressure her," Eliza whispers.

Heat creeps up my cheeks.
"Thanks, but I'll stay with Teagan."

"*Boring*," Joshua says,
snatching the bag from Ana Maria.

The setting sun is a blood orange,
the desert awash in pulpy juice
as Bailey and Co. wash down
the shriveled stems and caps
with bottled green smoothies.

They don't even try to hide.
The only thing watching
is a faded plaster statue of a coyote
giving them two thumbs up.

Reclining uneasily in a pool chair,
I watch them amble toward the jawbone
of purple mountains in the distance
while Teagan cuts through the water.

My phone buzzes again,
the same Portland number.
This time, I pick up.

"Crosby?"

Not a voice I know well,
but one I recognize instantly.

I force out a "yes?" and wait for the shadow
I hear in Bear's tone to creep closer.

"It's Deva," he says, just as the mountains
devour the sun.

DEATH ITSELF

casts no shadow.
You cannot hear it,
not even in the creak
of carriage wheels
or the click of
a midnight stranger's
foot on your doorstep.
You cannot see it,
just the shells and pelts
it leaves behind.
You cannot feel it
in your blood,
in your breath,
in your bone marrow.
What you feel is
sickness, and sickness
you can fight.
You can fight it
but you don't.
Deva, why
didn't you fight?

NOTHING CAN PREPARE YOU FOR THIS

Before passing the phone to Deva,
    Bear tells me in his honey-hive voice

that she isn't able to respond,
    and in that moment of uncertainty

where I don't know if the receiver
    is pressed against her ear,

where I'm in the kind of nightmare
    where you forget your monologue,

I feel more performance anxiety
    than grief, my hand shaking

as I walk to the peeling metal railing
    separating the pool patio from the desert.

My eyes shut tight as I imagine
    I could cut Malachite from the sky

like a tumor, as I discordantly whisper,
    "hi Deva," and "thank you for

everything you taught me," and
    "I'll see you in the fourth dimension"—

my levity sounding more like sarcasm,
    my thumb slipping down

to end the call, because that, at least,
    is one thing I can control.

NEED

I need to not
be in my head
right now.

Leaving Teagan
to her laps, I run
toward the setting sun.

Sandeep and Eliza
are lying down,
watching the stars
infect the dark.

Ana Maria and Joshua
are ambling down an arroyo,
laughingly screaming,
"I'm melting, I'm melting!"

Bailey sits by himself,
doodling in the sand
with a rusty piece of rebar.

My breath a sandstorm
scouring my lungs,
I pant, "Do you have
any more shrooms?"

BAILEY SEES

something feral in my eyes,
and doubt flickers through his.
"Have you done this before?"

"Of course," I say, the lie
smooth as the lukewarm juice
that washes the cryptlike
taste from my molars.

He watches me chew, choke, swallow.
Watches my mouth become a grave
I must claw myself out of.

"Be forewarned," he says. "This batch is—"
he mimics an accelerating engine
and airplanes his hand toward the moon,

but the vessel has left the atmosphere
without me—I feel hideously the same.

It's not working.

FUCK

it's working

EVERY BREATH A BEGINNING

it starts like screen fatigue   or a pink wine hangover

like the corona around the moon   on a cloudy-ish night

warm temples   treacly tongue

it starts with everything   feeling so good

with my boots coming off   and the sand   like satin

like a cat's back arching   up to meet my feet

like bailey   handing me the rebar   the ribbed metal

so salty-good i could stick it   in my mouth

but instead i draw   a bad circle   a cancerous cell   a planet

with an impact crater   from another planet

it starts   with bailey reminding me to breathe   with oxygen

orgasming into my lungs   it starts again

with every breath   a beginning   it starts

with bailey's skin so thin   i can see his whole

circulatory system   i can see   the electric wiring

of the whole universe   the lines that connect us

to the empty juice bottle   the flickering motel sign   the web

of light

with bailey at the center like a spider   it starts

with me saying   *i don't mean to alarm you*

but you are a prism   and bailey nodding   because he understands it starts   with him spooning me   with me unable

to stop talking because   my voice is a falcon flung skywards

a fishing line cast   into deep deep water

my voice is whatever   i want it to be   my voice is clay

that i can shape   my hands   my heart   my mouth   my heart

it starts   with me laughing   because this   *this*

is the kind of transcendence   i've been trying

to achieve   this is what it feels like   to watercolor-bleed

off your own margins   and fuck   *fuck*   it begins

all over again   every time i think it's over   because time

isn't real   isn't linear   and there will always

be this moment   wrapped in the arms   of a boy breathing

into my grandma hair   there will always be a time   before

malachite

before deva   before shannon   before my parents

met at a crosby stills & nash show   it starts

with me crying   without realizing   i am crying

face wet   eyes streaming   chest heaving   with sobs

something primal   something mucus   something ugly

trying to get out of me   it starts   with bailey saying

it's okay   and it starts   oh god

with me believing him

COMING DOWN

"Hey," Bailey says.
"Hey, remember to breathe."

I breathe. Just like he taught me
when I was learning how to run.

My soul is re-roosting in my body,
the satiny desert turning back to sand.

"That brought up some deep stuff for you,"
Bailey says. "Are you okay?"

I breathe, and my breath becomes
the sound of Deva's last gasps.

And then the words are pouring out,
and I'm telling Bailey everything

I've been bottling up and distilling
like an herbal tincture since I met her,

how I should've called 911,
should've made her get chemo,

should've known there are some things
good vibes and turkey tail can't cure.

Bailey blankets me in his limbs,
holds me close to his heartbeat.

"You can't save someone
who doesn't want to be saved."

He's right, and I'm not even mad.
He's allowed to be right, just this once.

As I reach automatically
for salty retorts that aren't there,

as I close my eyes and sink
into a psychedelic screensaver,

I finally understand how Bear
learned to love the whole world.

THE CHAIN

"I don't understand," I say later,
when my mind and sinuses have cleared.
"That felt almost . . . spiritual."

It's fully dark now, moon- and motel-light
guiding Bailey's friends back to their rooms.
He waves them past, says not to wait for us.

I feel empty but in a clean way,
dizzy but in a carousel way,
confused but in a cliffhanger way.

"There's a podcast I want to share with you,"
Bailey says. "About having religious experiences
without religion. It literally changed my life.

Religion is about control. *Thou shalts* and *thou shalt nots.*
Don't eat shellfish, don't wear polyester.
I don't think people want that.

I think people want to feel—"
he gestures at me,
"—whatever the fuck that was."

I think about all the rules I live by,
a choke chain getting tighter
even when I don't resist.

So resist, a voice in my head hisses.
But I'm afraid of what will happen
if I break the chain.

PROTEST

I'm not ready to go back
to my smoky non-smoking room,

so we walk to a 24-hour grocery store
for snacks and seltzers.

A camo-jacketed man in the parking lot
holds up a sign that says:

God Sent Malachite
Leviticus 18:22

Bailey doesn't say anything,
but his shoulders tighten.

The man's smirking eyes
travel down my pagan-core tunic

and up Bailey's coral-colored
skinny jeans.

I'm not like you,
I want to scream.

But haven't I waved my own
hateful signs? Haven't I

claimed that Malachite will kill
anyone with different beliefs?

"Want to keep walking?" I ask Bailey.
"I'm actually not that hungry."

JANUARY THIRD

dawns, 58 degrees and cloudless.

Like any other morning,
I shower and brush my teeth.

I put on my moon phase dress,
amethyst pendant, and black lipstick.

I clean my glasses. I comb
my page-white hair behind my ears.

I text my family that I'm safe
and that I love them.

I do all these things
for the last time.

HOPE AND FEAR ARE THE SAME THING

The TV in the motel lobby is playing news coverage
of the "Malachite mania" sweeping the nation—
aerial views of jam-packed campsites,
real-time trackers of the rogue planet's trajectory.

These projections look totally different
from the ones I follow on the dark web.
Malachite swooping like a smile
toward and away from Earth.

As I eat an orange that tastes like
orange-flavored toilet cleaner,
I scare myself by wishing for Malachite
to frown off course and obliterate us.

I flash back through a thousand summer nights
with Shannon, decoding our stars and cards and dreams.
I've built my life around predictions.
If I'm wrong about this, I don't know who I am.

THREE OF SWORDS

"You seem different today," Teagan observes
as we're filling a bucket with ice. "Calmer."

Strangely enough, I am. Last night I cried
until I couldn't see straight, cried until
the swords in my heart slid free.

I've given everything I had,
done everything I could.
The rest is up to Malachite.

One way or another,
it will all be over soon.

IN FIVE HOURS

we'll be in Tucson.
As we drive, I scroll
through my text history
with Shannon.

It's been three days
since I linked her
to a video about how
the mainstream media
is using fake science
to subdue mass panic.

It's been eight weeks
since I asked her
how she was.

MEANINGLESS

As the world flattens, the sky expands.
Suspended in the ceilingless blue,
Malachite is as round as the O in omen.

Not everything is an omen, Crosby.
Not everything means something.
Weren't those the words Shannon used

to break my heart? Then why do they
smooth out the turbulence in my mind?
Why does it feel so good, so peaceful

to imagine a world where,
instead of a harbinger of death,
four magpies are just four magpies.

LIKE A GIFT

clouds tumble up   over the dusty blue mountains

release a curtain of rain   we can see coming

from miles away

Bailey rolls down   the windows

when it hits   and we shriek   wild and alive

as petrichor and warm storms   rush through us

not an omen   good or bad   just a reminder

that life   like the weather   is unpredictable

SAGUARO NATIONAL PARK

is strangely familiar, even though
I've never been farther south
than San Francisco.

It's not the cacti—
chain-fruit cholla
and Spanish bayonet
and claret cup
and prickly pear—

and it's not the flowers—
brittlebush
and fairy duster
and scorpionweed
and velvet mesquite.

It's not the subdued palette
of sage-green,
pollen-yellow,
sunbaked-brown.

It's not the double rainbow
fading over the visitor center
or the clusters of green balloons
streaked with evaporating rainwater.

It's the sprawl of tents,
the constellations of campfires,
the air quivering with guitar chords
and children's laughter.

One whiff of hickory smoke,
one lick of a familiar folk song,
and I'm back at the Sunspirit Festival
where it all began.

HIGH CALORIE, LOW FREQUENCY

It's three in the afternoon by the time we roll up to our campsite.
Two and a half hours until sunset.
Seven hours, according to my sources,
    until the end of life as we know it.

I stand off to the side while Bailey and Teagan
    and the others set up the tents and telescopes,
wanting to make myself useful but not knowing
    how to move, how to breathe.

"You're meeting a friend here, right?"
    Bailey asks. "Sharon? Cheryl?"
"Shannon," I say, the syllables cutting
    the air like a crow's wings.

I scan the campsite for a flicker of her red hair,
    but she could be anywhere
in the park's 90,000 acres,
    enjoying her last few hours without me.

"She's not here yet," I lie, fishing a beer from the cooler.
    I'm not thirsty, but I need something to do
with my hands. Something to stop me
    tearing myself apart with anxiety.

"Shouldn't you eat something?" Teagan asks.
    Yes, Mom, I should, but I didn't pack
any organic unsalted cashews or seaweed snacks,
    and there's nothing in the cooler I can eat.

My stomach roars louder than the fire
    as Teagan spreads no-stir peanut butter
and high-fructose strawberry jam
    on Pepperidge Farm sourdough.

I've trained my mind to see these ingredients
        as chemicals, but my body isn't so discerning.
Saliva floods my mouth at the first bite
        of the first real food I've had in days.

Wordlessly, Teagan hands me a shiny bag
        of sour cream & onion–flavored potato chips,
and I devour those too, each crinkle-cut crisp
        tasting like the life I could've had.

I CAN'T STOP CHECKING THE TIME

3:48 p.m.

Ana Maria and Eliza go hiking.
Joshua endeavors to get day-drunk.
Sandeep tracks Malachite's path on his tablet.
Bailey adjusts his telescope's eyepiece.
Teagan tunes her guitar.
I toss scruffs of grass into the fire.

4:32 p.m.

Ana Maria and Eliza come back with a deer skull.
Joshua is successfully sloshed.
Sandeep announces Malachite's distance in kilometers.
Bailey invites me to look through the telescope; I shake my
head, teeth clenched.
Teagan is making friends with the 2.5-kid Iowan family at the
next campsite.
With my thumbnail, I pry a bottle cap from the hard-packed
dirt and toss it into the fire.

5:50 p.m.

All but the Western horizon is drenched in darkness.
A few campsites away, someone sets off fireworks until the park
rangers intervene.
An unleashed dog steals Ana Maria's deer skull.
Teagan plays guitar and leads a sing-along—*the sun is a mass of
incandescent gas.*
My nails scrape the ground.
I've run out of things to burn.

AND THEN I HEAR IT

Elusive and unmistakable
as the trill of a rare bird.

Hesitant and lovely as a trillium
opening to the green-steeped
sunlight in the forest's heart.

Achy as an almost-healed,
self-inflicted wound.

Shannon's laugh.

SHANNON NICOLE COLLINS

is walking toward the bathrooms
    with a girl I don't recognize
        but immediately hate,
            then hate myself for hating.

I stand up, nearly hitting
    my head on Malachite.
        It's close enough to suck
            the breath from my lungs.

Shannon's name tears from my mouth,
    and she—my ride(on broomsticks)-or-die,
        my neighbor of thirteen years,
            the Gemini to my Sagittarius,
                the full moon to my eclipse—

flinches.

Saguaro National Park, evening. CROSBY, some kind of eco-goth or whatever, takes a flying leap over a campfire and runs up to SHANNON, a redhead dressed boringly in a jean skirt and blue tank top.

SHANNON
Crosby? I . . . did you . . . what are you doing here?

CROSBY
(wringing her hands)
Hey. Hi. Sorry, I should've told you I was coming. It was kind of a last-minute thing.

Awkward pause.

CROSBY
Where are you staying?

SHANNON
(gestures)
Over there.

CROSBY
Is your boyfriend with you?

SHANNON
(shuffles her feet, looks away)
Um, yeah.

Awkward-er pause.

SHANNON'S FRIEND
I'm gonna go pee.

Awkward-est pause.

SHANNON
(turning back to CROSBY)
Sorry, I'm just . . . really surprised to see you here. Aren't you supposed to be at that party thing?

CROSBY
(muttering)
The Launch Party. Yeah, no. I changed my mind. Seeing you was
more important.

SHANNON
So do you still think . . . ?

SHANNON gestures at the sky, where a massive green planet is
slowly approaching.

CROSBY
I don't fucking know.
(laughs humorlessly)
Fuck.
(wipes her eyes)

SHANNON
Crosby, are you . . . ?

CROSBY
I'm sorry. I should go. I shouldn't have come.

CROSBY exits stage left.

SHATTERED

That *look*. That *look* she gave me.
Like I'm a bomb she doesn't know how to defuse.
Like she doesn't want to be anywhere
within a 50-mile radius
when I detonate.

I'm a fucking shameful mess
of a second-rate sideshow psychic,
preaching enlightenment
while my own chakras gutter out,
preaching connectedness
while I push everyone away.

Heedless of direction,
I push through the crowds until
the tents fall away, and I find myself
on a red-rock outcropping
overlooking an ancient seafloor
tombstoned with saguaros.

Malachite follows my every step,
inescapable as my own mind.

THE REASON WHY

I can't bring myself to look at her
when she lowers herself next to me,
but I know the particular smell
of her skin on a warm evening,
the cool blue sweetness
of her coconut conditioner.

"You didn't have to follow me,"
I mumble, picking at my nail polish.
"I know you moved across the country
just to get away from me."

She sighs. "Do you really think that?"

"I mean, it's pretty obvious.
Especially when you didn't come home
for Thanksgiving or Christmas.
And that interview you did . . . "

A sharp inhale. "You found that?"

I peel off a whole nail's worth
of black varnish. "You think
I'm stupid and pathetic.
Easy prey for conspiracies.
You think I'm like those
Westboro Baptist Church psychos
shouting that God sent Malachite
to kill all the gay people."

"Crosby."

I look up. And freeze. She's wearing
the malachite earrings she bought
all those months ago at Sunspirit.

"You're not the reason I left home."

Now it's her turn to look away.
"I didn't know how to tell you,"
she says, "about my brother."

IT MAKES TERRIBLE SENSE

Why she always wanted
to come over to my house,

why the runes she created
were to keep him out of her room,

why she didn't think it was funny
when we caught him pawing
through her underwear drawer,

why she didn't think
I'd understand.

THE ASTROPHYSICS OF GRIEF

"It didn't work," Shannon says. "The runes. The hexes.
But you believed so strongly that they did.
And I knew if I told you, you'd just
try some new curse or whatever."

She removes an earring, strokes her thumb
across its glossy green swirls, puts it back in.
"I didn't need witchcraft. I needed *you*."

I see myself as if from space,
a slow-motion explosion
of molten debris,
total obliteration
in total silence.

"I'm so sorry," I whisper.
"Shannon. I'm so sorry."

We're both crying,
both dispersing
through the galaxy,
our center of gravity
crushed to dust.

"I should have been there for you,"
I say, ashamed to have claimed
I was trying to save her, when really
I was trying to save myself.

Shannon isn't sentimental.
Her tears have already dried
in the arid Tucson breeze.

"Well, you're here now," she says.

I have to believe that particles
traveling alone through space
can find each other again.

I have to believe they can form
a new and brighter planet.

at the stroke of midnight, I shook Shannon awake
and lured her into the highest boughs of her apple tree,

assuring her the dark arcana of the witching hour
would gift us with the power of flight.

I can still hear her scream as she landed
with bone-splintering force.

I've always been pushing her higher.
Now it's my chance to lead her safely down.

FLYING LESSONS

When we descend the rocky ridge,
the campground is once again
smoke-choked and fizzling with fireworks,
but there is no haze thick enough,
no light bright enough
to obscure Malachite.

Stone of small doses.
Stone of deep healing.
Stone of long distances
crossed one step at a time.

Shannon moves deerlike
down the rocks,
my graceful acrobat,
my lost-and-found
everything.

I used to think of her as my acolyte,
but I have so much to learn from her.

How to walk away from the damage
without letting it define you.
How to grow a new life
from barren red soil.

All this time,
Shannon was the one
who knew how to fly.

LIKE A ROGUE PLANET

Bailey emerges from the crowd
to grab my hand and drag me
back to our campsite,
where Sandeep is shouting
a countdown of Malachite's
closest pass to Earth,
kilometers blazing
down to the bone,
and Teagan is looking
at the firmament
the way I looked at Shannon
when she gave me a second chance,
and Ana Maria and Eliza
are debating what this means
for the *Sailor Moon* franchise,
and Joshua—six beers deep—
is snoring into a bag
of Jet-Puffed marshmallows,
and Bailey's telescope
is waiting, naked,
for me.

WITHIN REACH

My heart orbits my chest as Bailey

     parks me in front   of the first and last

        telescope   I'll ever use.

"This is as close as it gets,"   he says. "It's now

or never."   The words

     of the time-freezing spell   rise like bile

under my tongue,   but the look Shannon gives me

     is fresh-shaved ginger root,   fresh-squeezed lemonade

settling my stomach.

       Looking through the eyepiece

is like going underwater,   my vision swimming

with phosphorus green,

     a brocaded palmist's tent,   an empty sleeping bag,

a phone with no voicemails,   a fever dream of bloody teeth,

      an amethyst buried in sand,   a dark web imageboard,

an overflowing litter box, a plane in freefall,

      a smoke-shrouded trampoline,

a whole planet in flames—

     Bailey wraps an arm   around my shaking shoulders.

"Remember to breathe," he says.

TRANSCENDENCE

My eyes are closed.
    I don't remember
        when I closed them.
            I don't remember
              who I am
                  without this fear.
                     But then the hand
                        I crossed the country
                            to hold one last time
                                twines its fingers
                                    through mine,

and I know
  it isn't the last time,
    and *I am transcending*
      friction, I am
        transcending pain,
      and I am
        opening my eyes,
                  and

PREMONITION

Yes.

This is the place.

The place the world will end

and begin again.

AUTHOR'S NOTE

Though *Meet Me in the Fourth Dimension* is a work of fiction, it was directly inspired by the misinformation pandemic running parallel to COVID-19. Long before the virus hit, we were already occupying different, algorithmically curated realities on social media. Lockdowns drove us deeper into these politically charged online spaces, where competing ideas of "the truth" pulled us even further apart.

With so much uncertainty surrounding our political and public health leadership, it's unsurprising that many people turned to conspiracy theories as a way to make sense of all the unrest and dysfunction in the world. Mind-controlling microchips in vaccines, a cabal of lizard people behind the Democratic Party, Donald Trump as a holy savior of humanity . . . this is just a sampling of the conspiracies running rampant across the Internet. To some, they may sound silly and easily dismissed. But to many, they were not only the capital-T Truth, but also worth sacrificing friendships and family over.

In July of 2020, I began writing *Meet Me in the Fourth Dimension* as a way to process the effects of this ideological cataclysm on my own relationships. I chose to write from the perspective of a conspiracy theory victim to help make sense of how misinformation divides us and how we can bridge those divides.

At the same time, Crosby's story is my own. Growing up, I was taught—directly and indirectly—to be distrustful of trends, group activities, and authority figures. My family rejected mainstream beliefs in favor of New Age occultism and natural medicine. Tarot and astrology were my lifeline when, as a teenager, I was recovering from an eating disorder. My spirituality gave me something bigger to believe in when I felt disconnected from my peers and disappointed with the limitations of reality.

In college, I made friends who challenged me to think critically about my beliefs. At first, I felt attacked, but the more I tried to defend myself, the more I saw the gaps in my perspective. Crosby goes through a similar arc of spiritual self-discovery, a painful but necessary crisis of faith.

Though my relationship to spirituality is much more complicated now, I'm deeply grateful to the community I grew up in and the knowledge I've gained from studying New Age mysticism. In *Meet Me in the Fourth Dimension*, I wanted my representation of Crosby's beliefs to be equal parts generous and critical. What helps her find meaning and beauty in the world is also what makes her susceptible to predatory conspiracy theories. Like the real people who consume and spread disinformation, she's a complex product of media and cultural influences.

Meet Me in the Fourth Dimension is a book about how our deeply held convictions can turn us against each other. It is also a book about friendship, forgiveness, and the transformation that can happen when we open our hearts and minds to other perspectives.

For those who have not been personally affected by conspiracies, I hope this book illuminates the devastating consequences of misinformation. For those who have, I hope there is resonance and solace in these pages. Writing Crosby's story allowed me to grieve, rage, and heal, and I hope in sharing it I can help others do the same.

ACKNOWLEDGMENTS

Meet Me in the Fourth Dimension challenged me creatively, intellectually, and emotionally more than anything I've written before or since. Without the support of some incredible people who believed in me when this project and the circumstances that inspired it felt hopeless, I'd probably still be in bed eating Ben & Jerry's and crying at the Taylor Swift documentary.

To my phenomenal agent Savannah Brooks, where to even start? Literally every single day of my life I'm overwhelmed with gratitude that you're on this journey with me. You saw the potential in this project when it was still heavily annotated with "I'm not actually going to write this! It's too painful!" and encouraged me to write it anyway. You rooted for Crosby even at her messiest. With your guidance and laser-sharp editorial insights, this book is the strongest version of itself. You are the best champion a girl could ask for. You're also just, like, one of the coolest people I know.

Profound gratitude to the editorial, production, design, and marketing teams at Page Street for bringing *Meet Me* to life. To my editor Tamara Grasty, your enthusiasm for this project made my day, my week, my year. Thank you for believing in Crosby's story and elevating it to a higher dimension. To Emma Hardy, thank you for the shroomy, dreamy artwork that so beautifully captures the spirit of the book. Kumari Pacheco, I'm so grateful for your thoughtful and razor-sharp copy edits. You all have given this book such a wonderful and supportive home.

To my dear, dear friends Robin Cedar and Kayla Pearce, words cannot express how much I adore and appreciate you. You always know what I'm trying to say and help me say it better. You're generous with your praise but don't let me get away with anything. When I thought this book would kill me, you helped me laugh through the pain. I am so freaking lucky to have you both as readers, friends, and RPG companions. In both real life and Dungeons & Dragons, there's no one I'd rather have fighting by my side.

To Sarah Boyle, Rachel Dean, Madeline Ormenyi, and Madeline Stevens, a tidal wave of love for your enthusiastic response to the first batch of poems I wrote for *Meet Me*. This was an intensely vulnerable project, and you all gave me the safety and support I needed to finish drafting. And to Sarah, who read the completed draft, thank you for helping me achieve my lifelong dream of making a reader cry. Sorry not sorry. [smiling devil emoji]

To the Literary Liaisons group, thank you for welcoming me into your workshop when I moved to DC, and for being a source of top-tier feedback and delicious snacks all these years. This community has been such a pillar of stability for me throughout some major life changes.

To my little sisters Dulcie and Sorrel, just WOW. The pandemic tried so hard to tear our family apart, but it only brought us closer together. I know I'm the court jester and not the sappy one, but I am so proud of the strong, thoughtful, empathetic adults you've become. Thank you for reality-checking me as I processed particulars of our New Age childhood and for offering your perspective on the social and spiritual issues this book grapples with. I love you both very much and I'm sorry for yelling at you so much when you were kids. But tbh you were very annoying.

To my parents, from the early days of reading me *Go, Dog. Go!* to the moment I got to call you about this book deal, you've always been my biggest supporters. If you were panicking when I announced I was going to grad school for poetry, you did a great job of hiding it. I have three decades of adventures to thank you for, but I'm particularly grateful for the aura of humor and whimsy that followed us wherever we moved. You taught me that the sacred and the silly can happily coexist, and that my voice is big enough to contain both. I wrote this book in that same spirit. I hope it can shine a light through the darkness.

To my husband Peter, I don't know what kind of magical nonsense this is, but after thirteen years together we're still in our honeymoon phase. I do know that no small part of the magic comes from how you challenge me to think critically about myself, my beliefs, and the world, and that this book wouldn't exist without our deep exploration of each other's minds. Thank you for being the Bailey to my Crosby, the method to my madness, and the one who remembers to unplug the modem every night.

And to you, reader, thank you for spending time with these poems. It means more to me than you could ever know.

ABOUT THE AUTHOR

Rita Feinstein is the author of the poetry collections *Life on Dodge* and *Everything is Real*. Her work has appeared in *Willow Springs*, *Sugar House*, *Salamander Magazine*, and *The Normal School*, among other publications, and has been nominated for Best of the Net and Best New Poets awards. She received her MFA in Poetry from Oregon State University, and now teaches creative writing to kids and teens in Washington, DC. She lives with her husband, who is a lawyer, and her dog, who is not.